FOREVER AND ALWAYS SERIES - BOOK 1

THE *Lies* WE LIVE BY

NORA BLOOM

Chapter One

LISA

Lisa Montgomery's hand hesitated on the worn brass handle of Maggie's Tavern, her pulse thrumming in her ears like the distant roll of ocean waves. With a deep breath that did little to steady her nerves, she pushed the door open, stepping into the dimly lit refuge that hummed with the life of the small Alaskan town called Mapletown. The scent of aged wood and toasted hops wrapped around her, as comforting as a well-worn blanket, and for a moment, it eased the tightness in her chest.

You can do this, Lisa. You can start over. People do it all the time.

Her hazel eyes, wide with a mix of apprehension and curiosity, flitted across the room. They were searching, seeking out the fiery crown of curls that belonged to Maggie, the woman who had given Lisa this chance at a fresh start. Her gaze passed from face to friendly face, each patron lost in their world of laughter and conversation—a tableau of community that Lisa longed to be part of yet felt so disconnected from.

And then, like a lighthouse piercing through the fog of her nervousness, there was Maggie. The woman stood behind the bar, her red hair a vibrant contrast to the backdrop of polished bottles and gleaming glasses. Each movement Maggie made seemed to carry the rhythm of the place within it, the very heartbeat of the establishment pulsating under her command.

Lisa's heart skipped, catching up to the beat as she wove through the tables toward the bar. Her hair, usually a cascade of controlled waves, felt wilder here, perhaps an echo of her inner tumult as she neared her new employer.

"Hi," Lisa said, her voice a soft melody that threaded through the ambient noise.

Maggie turned, her weathered yet kindly face breaking into a wide smile that reached her eyes. Those sharp and discerning eyes seemed to take Lisa in whole—her gentle demeanor, her hopeful stance, the way she clutched her purse like a lifeline. Yet there was no judgment there, only the warmth of acceptance.

"Welcome aboard, Lisa!" Maggie exclaimed, her voice rich with genuine cheer. "We're thrilled to have you with us. It's gonna be exciting to have new energy around the place."

Lisa's lips curved upward, responding almost

reflexively to Maggie's infectious enthusiasm. In that simple exchange, the weight she carried on her slender shoulders seemed to lighten just a fraction, igniting a spark of excitement within her reserved nature.

"Thank you, Maggie. I can't wait to get started," Lisa replied, her words colored with a sincerity that mirrored the hope flickering in her heart. It was the beginning of something new, the first step into a world where she could weave herself into the fabric of these people's lives, one smile, one kind gesture at a time. And where—most importantly—no one would know who she was.

Maggie's hand swept through the air like a seasoned conductor directing an orchestra, her gesture summoning a young woman from the other side of the bar.

"Lisa, meet Sarah—she's one of our best. She'll make sure you're up to speed in no time," she said, her voice warm and reassuring.

"Hey, there!" Sarah bounded over with an energy that seemed to bubble up from an inexhaustible spring. Her freckled face broke into a wide grin, and her short black hair bobbed as she halted beside Lisa. "Welcome to the crew! Don't worry about a thing; stick with me, and you'll be fine. This town might seem quiet, but it's full of characters. Just wait until you meet them all!"

"Thank you, Sarah," Lisa responded, her eyes lighting up with gratitude. The younger waitress's friendliness was infectious, and Lisa felt a surge of relief at the thought of having such a guide.

"First tip," Sarah whispered conspiratorially, leaning in close enough for Lisa to catch a hint of her floral perfume, "always refill Mr. Henderson's bourbon before he asks. He's a sweetheart, but he likes his drinks flowing constantly."

Lisa nodded, logging the information away as vital, her smile still firmly in place. She turned slightly to take in the rest of the room, allowing the vibrant chatter and clinking of glasses to wash over her. It was a symphony of small-town life, each note played by a familiar face, each harmony a shared history.

Her gaze drifted across the patrons, absorbing their ease and camaraderie, when she caught sight of him—Oliver Thompson. He sat at the bar, his posture relaxed, a glass cradled in his calloused hands that spoke of hard work and long days at sea. His deep blue eyes, reminiscent of the Alaskan waters he navigated, flickered toward her, and for a heartbeat, the clamor around her dimmed. She had met him the day before on the dock when she had just arrived and spoken to him briefly. The way he looked at her—and did again now—made her blush.

Recognition sparked in his gaze, brief but unmistakable, before he returned to the animated discussion with his friend, Mark. The broad-shouldered lumberjack guffawed at something Oliver said, his head thrown back in mirth, while Oliver smiled, his lips curving in a way that reached his eyes, making them crinkle at the corners.

Lisa's heart thrummed with a mixture of curiosity and caution. Those few seconds of eye contact had stirred something within her—a flutter of connection in this tapestry of new faces and stories. She made a mental note of Oliver's presence, aware that in a town so tightly knit, paths were bound to cross again.

The warmth of the room embraced her, and the trepidation that had accompanied her arrival began to melt into budding anticipation. Here, in the hum of Maggie's bar, among these people who seemed to embrace life with open arms, Lisa sensed the possibility of fresh starts and unexpected friendships. It was both heartwarming and exciting, and she allowed herself to bask in that feeling, even if just for a moment.

The chime of the door signaled another entry into the cozy realm of Maggie's bar, but Lisa barely registered it as she glided between the tables with a tray balanced expertly in her hand. A natural at adapting to new environments, she found herself falling into the rhythm of service with surprising ease. She delivered a frothy-topped pint of beer to an eager patron, her smile unwavering even as her mind worked to memorize faces and favorite drinks.

"Thank you, darlin'," an elderly man with a face like weathered leather beamed up at her. His twinkling eyes crinkled with genuine delight as he took his order from her steady hands.

"Enjoy," Lisa replied, her tone warm, touched by the endearing interactions that felt woven into the fabric of this place.

She absorbed the snippets of conversation that floated around her—tales of fishing ventures gone awry, playful banter over the day's catch, and the occasional burst of laughter that erupted like a geyser from the heart of the room. Each story seemed to cling to her, a mosaic of lives lived boldly beneath the Alaskan sky.

Her circuit brought her near the bar again, where a shift in the crowd gave way to a clear view of Oliver Thompson. He leaned comfortably against the polished wood, the light catching the subtle stubble along his jaw. As if sensing her gaze, he turned, and their eyes met once more. This time, however, he pushed off the bar and approached her. His gait was easy, each step deliberate, closing the distance with the confidence of a man used to navigating unpredictable tides.

"Hey, there," he said, his voice carrying the lilt of someone who had seen many seasons pass in this town. "You're picking things up pretty fast."

The friendly smile accompanying his words threatened to disassemble the walls she'd carefully built around herself.

"A girl's gotta do what a girl's gotta do," she responded, matching his smile with one that reached her eyes, though she maintained a guarded softness about her. "It's been a good first day so far."

"First days can tell you a lot about a place," he mused, resting an elbow on an empty table. "You never told me when I asked you yesterday at the dock. How did you find this town? And why this place? Where did you come from?"

Lisa paused, a glass in hand, the question dangling in the air between them like a challenge. She could feel the weight of her past pushing against the words that would come easiest. Instead, she chose the ones that kept her secrets just that—secret.

"I was... I was just looking for a change of scenery," she said lightly, her gaze flitting away momentarily.

"Ah, the elusive 'change of scenery,'" Oliver chuckled, his eyes not missing the slight shift in her demeanor. "Well, whatever your reasons, you've got a knack for making people feel welcome. That's a rare thing."

"Thank you," she replied, her cheeks warming slightly at the compliment.

"Anyway, I'll let you get back to it," he said, stepping back with a nod of respect for her boundaries. "But I hope we get the chance to chat again, Lisa."

"Maybe we will," she allowed, the hint of a promise lingering in her voice as she turned back to her duties, leaving Oliver watching her, the intrigue evident in his thoughtful gaze.

As Lisa continued her evening, weaving through the tables, refilling drinks, and exchanging pleasantries, she couldn't help but feel the threads of connection beginning to form, delicate yet persistent. And in the back of her mind, the echo of an invitation to open up hung in the balance, both heartwarming and frightening in its potential.

As the evening bore on, Lisa swept through the bar with an unassuming grace, her tray balanced effortlessly as she navigated between the rustic wooden tables. The patrons' laughter provided a boisterous backdrop to her silent ballet, and amidst the revelry, Oliver's voice soon called out to her again.

"Hey, Lisa," he beckoned, patting the empty stool beside him. "Got a minute?"

She approached, nodding to acknowledge his request. "Sure, what can I get for you?"

"Nothing right now, just some company," Oliver said with a gentle smile. He gestured toward the stool again, his invitation clear but unimposing.

Lisa hesitated for a fraction of a second—her instinct was to remain in motion, a specter of service rather than a participant in camaraderie. Yet something about Oliver's earnest expression encouraged her to pause. She perched on the edge of the stool, her posture attentive.

Oliver leaned forward, resting his elbows on the bar. "You know, this place has been the heart of our town since I was a boy. My dad used to bring me here after fishing trips. Said it was where all the good stories were caught." His deep blue eyes danced with the reflection of memories past.

Her lips curved upwards, intrigued by the glimpse into his life. "It seems like everyone has a story to share around here."

"True enough," he agreed, then paused, considering her. "You have a way of listening that makes people want to talk. It's not just about hearing the words; it's seeing them take shape in your eyes. Kinda like you're painting their tales in your mind."

She felt a blush rise to her cheeks but accepted the compliment with a nod. "Everyone needs someone to listen, don't they?" Her voice was soft, but there was a steel of conviction behind it.

"Absolutely." Oliver's gaze lingered on her for a moment longer before he continued. "You know, when I was ten, I caught my first king salmon right off the pier. Felt like I'd wrestled a sea monster. My old man was so proud that he had that fish mounted on the wall at home."

Lisa laughed, the sound mingling with the clinking of glasses and the murmur of voices. "That must've been quite the battle."

"Wasn't just the catch," Oliver explained. "It was sharing the triumph with my dad. That's what made it special."

Lisa's eyes softened and reflected the warmth of the tale. "Seems like those moments are the ones that stick with us," she mused aloud.

"Exactly. Maybe I can take you fishing one day soon. Show you what we have to offer around here."

Lisa smiled shyly, then turned her back to him. Oliver signaled Maggie for another round. As the night wore on, he shared more snippets of his life, and with each story, Lisa found herself more engaged, her questions thoughtful and encouraging.

"Did you ever think of leaving?" she asked at one point, her curiosity genuine.

"Sure, I thought about it," he admitted. "But this place has a hold on me. My roots are deep in this soil, in the ebb and flow of the tides."

Lisa glanced around the lively bar, understanding that sentiment more than she cared to admit. Her own roots had been severed, yet here she was, tentatively reaching out through the fertile ground of this small Alaskan town.

As the evening waned, she noticed how patrons would wait for her to pass by, eager to catch her attention and share a piece of their history or a fragment of their day. With each interaction, she offered a smile, her demeanor warm as the sun breaking through an overcast sky.

"Thank you for the advice," a young man said

after she recommended a particularly hearty dish to combat the chill outside.

"Anytime," Lisa replied, her smile unwavering.

"Your kindness is a breath of fresh air," an elderly woman commented, her wrinkled hands clasping Lisa's for a moment longer than necessary.

"Thank you, that means a lot," Lisa responded, the weight of gratitude apparent in her tone.

By the time most of the customers had left and the chairs were stacked atop the tables, Lisa had become a woven thread in the tapestry of the bar, her presence subtly essential. Oliver, who was the only one still left, watched her from across the room, admiration evident in his stance.

"Looks like you've made quite the impression tonight," he remarked as she passed by to clock out.

"Thanks to a welcoming crowd," she deflected with humility, yet the spark in her eyes acknowledged the shared victory.

"About that fishing trip—" Oliver began, the words hanging between them like an unfinished melody.

"Let's talk about it tomorrow," Lisa suggested, her voice laced with caution.

"Tomorrow," he agreed, nodding with a knowing smile, confident that the mysteries of Lisa Montgomery would slowly unfold like the petals of a rare and beautiful flower.

～

Lisa wiped down the mahogany surface of the bar on the second night working there, her movements rhythmic and sure. The clink of glasses and the soft murmur of conversations wrapped around her like a comforting quilt. She had listened more than she had spoken that night, her hazel eyes reflecting an empathy that seemed to draw out the guarded secrets of the patrons who sat before her.

"Never thought I'd find myself telling someone about the time I caught the 'big one' on Bear Creek," chuckled a burly fisherman, his weathered face breaking into a grin as he glanced at Lisa. "Guess you just have that way about you."

She merely nodded, her lips curving into the smile that had become a flare in the dim light of the bar. There was warmth in their words, a recognition that extended beyond simple pleasantries. Her reticence to discuss her past did not seem to matter here; it was her presence and her willingness to listen that filled the spaces between stories, laughter, and the occasional clatter of a dropped fork.

"Thank you for letting me be a part of your evening," Lisa said, her voice soft but resonant in the dwindling chatter as patrons began to don their coats and scarves.

"Part of their evening?" Sarah echoed with a playful roll of her eyes. "Honey, you're part of the town now."

As the last few customers filtered out into the night, cold air nipped at the doorway, causing Lisa to shiver slightly. She helped turn chairs upside down onto tables, her motions synchronized with those of her coworkers. In the quiet aftermath, she allowed herself a moment to reflect. The day's apprehension had melted away, replaced by something unexpectedly comforting—a burgeoning sense of place.

"Good night, Lisa," Maggie called out, her red curls bouncing as she disappeared into the back.

"Good night," Lisa replied, her words floating in the now-empty space.

With the bar silent and still, Lisa stood, absorbing the echoes of camaraderie, the remnants of laughter, the vestiges of connection. It was unfamiliar yet oddly reassuring, this feeling of belonging. She had never thought she would find that. A smile played at the corner of her mouth as she imagined the stories that awaited her, the histories woven into the fabric of this small Alaskan enclave. So many tales to hear, so many lives to touch with her unassuming grace.

Tugging her coat tighter around her shoulders, Lisa stepped out into the brisk Alaskan night, her heart quietly thrumming with the anticipation of all the tomorrows to come. She was no longer just a passing shadow; she was becoming a part of the heartbeat of this town—a gentle pulse in its sprawling wilderness. And as the stars blinked overhead, she knew that, despite everything, she had found a slice of home among the pines and the people of this tucked-away world.

The frosty air nipped at Lisa's cheeks as she wrapped her scarf a little tighter, the warmth of Maggie's bar still lingering in her bones. It was then that Oliver's strong voice broke through the chill, halting her in the glow of the neon sign.

"Lisa," he called out with an easy smile, his eyes reflecting the dim light as if they were part of the night sky itself.

She turned to face him, finding comfort in the familiar ruggedness of his features. The sea had etched its story into his skin, but it was his sincerity that shone through the most.

"Mind if I walk with you?"

She smiled, even if it was cautious. "Not at all."

"Your knack for listening... it's something special," Oliver began, his hands tucked into the pockets of his worn jeans. "You've got this way about you, makes folks feel heard. It's rare."

Lisa felt a blush warm her cheeks, not used to such open admiration. She offered a small, humble smile, her eyes briefly meeting his before dipping away.

"Thanks, Oliver. That means a lot, coming from you," she said, her voice soft yet clear in the night.

He nodded as if he understood her unspoken words, then leaned forward slightly, his excitement barely contained.

"So, I was wondering," he ventured, glancing back

toward the porch outside the closed convenience store where his friend Mark stood, giving him a supportive thumbs-up. "Mark and I are heading out on the river next weekend—doing a bit of fishing. We'd be honored if you joined us."

Her heart skipped, caught between the thrill of new adventures and the shadow of her past reservations. A fishing trip with these kindhearted locals—it was the sort of thing the old Lisa might have jumped at without a second thought.

"Oliver, that's really sweet of you. I'm touched by the invite," Lisa said, the words true and heavy on her tongue. But within her eyes, a flicker of hesitation danced—the silent guardian of her history.

"Look, no pressure," Oliver added quickly, reading the caution in her gaze. "Just thought it'd be nice to get to know you beyond the bar chatter. And," he paused, a playful edge to his voice, "maybe we'll even catch some fish if we're lucky."

A genuine laugh escaped Lisa's lips, and the weight of her secrets lifted for a moment.

"Maybe," she echoed, allowing herself the luxury of enjoying the thought.

"Anyway, think about it," Oliver concluded, stepping back. His gaze lingered on her, a mix of curiosity and respect threading through his expression.

"Goodnight, Oliver," Lisa said, her voice carrying a newfound strength.

With a nod and a wave that held promises of stories yet untold, she turned and walked toward the small house she had rented, leaving behind a trail of intrigue and the echo of her laughter.

Oliver watched her go with a thoughtful look etched on his face. There was more to Lisa Montgomery than met the eye, and he couldn't help but feel drawn to the mystery and resilience she carried. As the door closed behind her, her silhouette etched in his mind, he silently vowed to patiently unravel the enigma that was Lisa, one day at a time.

Chapter Two

OLIVER

ONE DAY EARLIER

The chill of the Alaskan morning clung to the air like a thin veil, the town slowly waking under the soft glow of the rising sun. Oliver Thompson stood outside his weathered fishing boat, his hands buried in the pockets of his thick woolen sweater as he surveyed the harbor's gentle bustle. He was a familiar fixture against the backdrop of swaying boats and fluttering gulls, his gaze as steady as the tides.

As he watched, the light caught on a figure moving gracefully among the throng of townsfolk. Her medium-length, wavy brown hair danced with the breeze, and her smile, as she exchanged brief pleasantries with passersby, seemed to brighten the muted colors of the dawn. The arrival of this woman was unexpected yet stirred something within Oliver that he couldn't quite name. Her warm eyes held stories untold, and her presence brought a new energy to the sleepy streets.

For a moment, Oliver simply observed, admiring the gentle way she carried herself as if she were a melody only he could hear amidst the symphony of the harbor. His curiosity, piqued by her enigmatic aura, urged him forward, boots thudding softly against the wooden pier.

"Morning," Oliver called out as he approached, his voice carrying over the sound of lapping water against the hulls.

"Morning," she said shyly. "Those are some big waves out there today. Must be brave to weather those."

"Oh, I'm no hero," he said, laughing. "Absolutely not. Just a plain fisherman like most people here. Nothing special."

"I see," she said and walked past him.

He followed her with his eyes, unable to stop looking at her. "I haven't seen you around before. Are you visiting or...?"

Lisa turned, her smile lingering like the last notes of a lullaby, "Actually, I just arrived last night."

"Are you just passing through?" he asked.

"I rented the small house over there on the corner," she said and pointed.

"Mr. Henderson's old house? It used to belong to his mother until she died last year. He grew up there. That house has seen a lot of this town's history."

"That's the one."

"So, you're planning on staying?" he asked hopefully.

She shrugged. "Looks like it."

"Welcome to our little corner of the world," Oliver said, his eyes reflecting the sincerity of his words. "I'm Oliver. If there's anything you need to know about this place, I'm your man."

"Thank you, Oliver," Lisa replied, a hint of gratitude weaving through her voice. "I'm Lisa. It's beautiful here—quiet, peaceful."

"Ah, it's got its moments," he chuckled warmly, rocking back on his heels. "What brings you to a remote spot like this? If you don't mind me asking."

Her eyes momentarily flickered, like the surface of the sea hiding depths beneath. "Just needed to try something new," she offered, her words floating on the wind.

"Can't argue with that. The views here have a way of growing on you," he mused, gesturing toward the mountains cradling the town. A sense of excitement bubbled within him, the kind that came from meeting someone who might just appreciate the raw beauty of the place as much as he did.

"Indeed, they do," she said, her gaze following his gesture, soaking in the grandeur of the rugged landscape.

"Anyway, if you're looking for recommendations —best coffee, freshest catch, or maybe the quietest spot to take it all in—I'd be happy to show you around," Oliver continued, hoping to see more of that captivating smile.

"That's very kind of you, Oliver," Lisa responded with a warmth to her words that suggested an opening, a willingness to explore these new surroundings and perhaps even new acquaintances. "I'm actually on my way to apply for work at the local tavern on Main Street."

"Ah, Maggie's Tavern. That's my favorite place," he said. "Heck, it's everyone's favorite place. Maggie is great. You'll like her. She'll take good care of you."

"I hope so. Everyone so far has been so kind," she said.

"Kindness is easy when the company's good," he said with an easy grin, feeling the promise of a heart-warming connection in the crisp morning air.

As soon as Oliver stepped into the dimly lit bar, the murmur of conversations washed over him. He made his way through the crowd, scanning the faces until he saw her behind the counter. Her wavy hair caught the soft light from the pendant lamps above, giving her a halo-like glow. How very fitting, he thought to himself.

Her eyes seemed lost in thought as she expertly served drinks and exchanged polite nods with customers. This was the seventh day in a row he had come here this week just to see her. Oliver didn't usually drink this much, but she was worth the effort, even if she kept refusing to meet with him outside of the tavern.

"Evening, Lisa," Oliver said, taking a seat at the bar. His voice had the familiar timbre of the sea—a soothing, rhythmic quality that was hard to ignore.

"Hello, Oliver," she replied without meeting his gaze, placing a coaster in front of him with a practiced hand.

"Rough day?" he ventured, trying to catch her eye as he ordered a drink.

"Something like that," she murmured, her smile not quite reaching her eyes.

Oliver noticed how she deflected, a subtle shift in her shoulders designed to steer the conversation away from herself. But her guarded nature only drew him in further, igniting a spark of curiosity about the woman who held so much back.

"Seems like you're settling in well here," he tried again, watching as she filled a pint glass with a deft tilt.

"Thanks to the friendly locals," Lisa conceded, allowing herself a brief glance in his direction.

"Any plans for your day off tomorrow? I know of a nice trail up north that offers a great view of the northern lights."

"Maybe," she said, her voice carrying an undertone of hesitation. "I haven't really thought about it."

"Mind if I join you if you decide to go?" Oliver

asked, the question hanging between them like a challenge.

"I would prefer to go alone," she responded softly, a clear message wrapped in gentle words.

"Fair enough," Oliver smiled, undeterred. "But the offer stands. This place has a lot of hidden gems, and I'd hate for you to miss out."

As the night wore on, Oliver found reasons to linger, sharing laughter and stories with other regulars, all the while keeping a casual watch over Lisa. He made small talk whenever she passed by, each word carefully chosen to chip away at the wall she'd built around herself.

"Beautiful evening, isn't it?" he'd comment as she wiped down the bar.

"Sure is," she'd reply, her guard momentarily lowered before she caught herself.

When closing time rolled around, Oliver helped stack chairs, their movements falling into a comfortable rhythm. She thanked him with a nod, her expression still a mask of polite distance.

"See you tomorrow, Lisa," Oliver called out as he left, his heart filled with a mixture of hope and anticipation.

"Goodnight, Oliver," she said, a hint of warmth finally breaking through the cool veneer.

As he stepped out under the vast Alaskan sky, the stars above mirrored the thrill of possibility within him. The night was alive with the promise of the unknown.

Chapter Three

The clink of glasses and the low hum of conversation filled the air as Lisa moved behind the bar, her movements fluid and practiced. Oliver, perched on his usual stool, watched with a quiet appreciation that had become familiar to her over the past few weeks. It was an ordinary Thursday evening, but something about it felt different to Lisa. She had been in town for four weeks and was settling in well, even if it took some getting used to the cold.

"Trying the new IPA tonight?" she asked, sliding a frosted glass toward him.

"Thought I'd take a walk on the wild side," Oliver grinned, his eyes sparkling with mirth.

Lisa chuckled, feeling the corners of her mouth lift in a way that was becoming less rare around him.

"Let me know if it's too wild for you."

"Will do. But hey, I noticed you humming earlier. You have a favorite band?"

Lisa hesitated, just for a moment, before the truth slipped out. "I'm a sucker for old jazz. Billie Holiday, Ella Fitzgerald...."

She trailed off, surprised by her own openness.

"Jazz, huh?" Oliver said, nodding thoughtfully. "There's something timeless about those tunes. They've got soul."

Her eyes met his, and she saw genuine interest there. Not the prying curiosity she'd grown so wary of but a shared spark of excitement over something as simple as a love for music.

"Ever since I was a kid," she found herself confessing. "My mom used to play their records. It's one of the few hobbies I've held onto."

"Music has a way of sticking with you," he replied, his voice softening with a tinge of nostalgia. "For me, it was stories. My granddad had a talent for spinning yarns about the sea. He'd talk of adventures, storms that raged like mythical beasts, and calm waters that reflected the stars. Made me dream of being a storyteller myself."

"Is that why you became a fisherman? For the stories?" Lisa asked, leaning in, her curiosity piqued.

"Partly," Oliver admitted, a wistful smile playing on his lips. "But also for the peace it brings. There's nothing like the silence of dawn on the water, waiting for the world to wake up."

Lisa observed the passion lighting up Oliver's

face and realized she was seeing a glimpse of the man beyond the rugged exterior—a man with dreams and reflections that resonated with her more than she expected.

"Sounds lonely," she commented, not without empathy.

"Sometimes," he conceded. "But then again, loneliness can be a friend if you get to know it well enough."

Their conversation ebbed and flowed like the tides he spoke of, with Lisa sharing snippets of her life between serving drinks and Oliver recounting tales that made her long for the sea. As the night progressed, the initial walls that stood between them crumbled, piece by piece, revealing the foundation for something new and unexpectedly thrilling.

As the last patrons filtered out into the chilly Alaskan night, Lisa caught herself hoping Oliver would linger just a little longer under the excuse of helping her close up. And when he did, offering a hand with a smile that no longer felt like a stranger's, she realized she was right where she wanted to be. At that moment, under the glow of the neon lights, they were two kindred spirits finding comfort in each other's company—a heartwarming connection blossoming amidst the excitement of newfound friendship and the whisper of potential romance.

Lisa wiped down the bar with a practiced hand, her movements almost automatic. The soft hum of the refrigerator blended with the distant howl of the wind outside. It was a quiet Tuesday evening, and the sparse scattering of locals had dwindled to just a few regulars huddled in their booths, nursing their drinks.

"Need any help with that?" Oliver's voice cut through the quiet, his tone casual but tinged with an unmistakable warmth.

She turned to find him leaning against the bar, his eyes reflecting a sincerity that reached out to her like a lifeline in rough seas. His offer to assist was habitual by now, a small tradition that had woven itself into their closing routine.

"Thanks, but I think I've got it," Lisa replied, her smile involuntary, the corners of her mouth lifting before she could catch them.

Something about Oliver made her feel at ease, a sensation she hadn't felt in a long time. His presence was comforting, like the steady lighthouse beam that guided ships safely home. But it also scared her. Falling for him wasn't on her agenda. This was not what she had planned.

"Okay," he said, pushing off from the counter with a shrug that didn't quite hide his disappointment. "But if you change your mind...."

"Actually, there is something," she hesitated, not used to asking for help. "The storeroom lightbulb went out. Could you...?"

"Say no more," he grinned, rolling up his sleeves

as he headed toward the back. And just like that, he was there for her again, ready to step in wherever needed without expecting anything in return.

Watching Oliver disappear into the storeroom, Lisa allowed herself a moment to truly look at him. The way his shoulders moved with confidence, the easy strength in his steps, and the laughter lines that crinkled around his eyes all spoke of a man who was as steady as the ground she stood on. She found herself appreciating the solidity he brought to her world, a world that had felt so precarious for so long.

"Got it!" Oliver announced triumphantly, emerging from the storeroom, the once-dark space now bathed in a warm glow. "You won't have to worry about that for a while."

"Thank you, Oliver," she said, her gratitude genuine. "You always seem to know when I need a helping hand."

"Speaking of hands," he began, a playful edge to his voice. "I was wondering if you might let me steal yours for an evening? Take you out on a date? Maybe dinner at the new place over on Maple Street? I hear their salmon is almost as good as the ones I catch."

Lisa paused, the unexpected invitation sending a ripple of excitement through her. She felt her pulse quicken, a sign that Oliver's presence was affecting her more than she cared to admit. Her cheeks flushed with a mix of surprise and anticipation.

"I... that's really kind of you," she stumbled over

her words, her heart fighting her head. "I'm not sure if I—"

"Hey, no pressure," he interjected smoothly, sensing her hesitation. "Just two friends enjoying a meal together. We can talk about the sea, the stars, or even the mysterious art of cocktail making." His chuckle was disarming, his gaze holding hers with gentle persuasion.

"Two friends," she repeated softly, letting the idea settle over her like a warm blanket. The thought of spending an evening with Oliver didn't just appeal to her; it felt right.

"Two friends," he confirmed, his smile hopeful yet patient.

"Okay," Lisa found herself saying, her own smile mirroring his. "Dinner sounds nice."

"Great!" Oliver's delight was palpable. "It's a date then. But, you know, the friend kind."

"Of course," she laughed, her laughter lighter than it had been in ages. In that simple exchange, a door opened to possibilities she'd never imagined, and for the first time in a very long time, Lisa Montgomery looked forward to what lay beyond. But it also scared her more than anything.

Chapter Four

The wind whispered through the pines as Lisa stood on her porch, arms wrapped around herself against the evening chill. Her breath formed small clouds that drifted lazily before dissipating into the Alaskan air. The last hints of daylight lingered on the horizon, painting the sky in soft hues of purple and orange.

"Beautiful, isn't it?" Oliver's voice broke the silence, his figure emerging from the twilight like a familiar spirit.

Lisa turned, her heart skipping a beat at the sight of him leaning against the wooden railing, a warm smile gracing his rugged features.

"It is," she agreed, though she was unsure if she referred to the sunset or the man watching it with her.

Oliver took a step closer, the planks creaking under his boots. His eyes seemed to reflect the fading light. "About dinner tomorrow," he began tentatively, "I was thinking—"

"Oliver," Lisa cut in, the words catching slightly in her throat. She clutched the edge of her cardigan tighter. "I've been giving it some thought, and I don't think it's a good idea."

His brow furrowed gently, concern etching his face. "Is it because of what I said? 'Cause if it's about calling it a date—"

"It's not that," Lisa hurried to explain, her eyes flitting away. "You've been nothing but kind. It's just... I'm not ready for anything more right now."

"Hey, no worries," Oliver assured her, his voice steady. He reached out, resting a calloused hand over hers on the porch railing. "We can take this as slow as you need. Friendship is a fine place to start."

Lisa felt a warmth in his touch that made her want to lean into it, into him. But she retreated a step, afraid of where that might lead. "I think it would be better if we just kept things simple."

"All right." He nodded, accepting her boundaries with a grace that only made him more endearing. "Simple it is."

As days passed, Oliver's presence in Lisa's life became an unspoken comfort, his persistence never crossing the line into presumption. And then, one brisk morning, she opened her door to find him standing there, a radiant bunch of wildflowers in his hands.

"Morning, Lisa," he greeted, the corners of his mouth lifting in a hopeful smile.

She blinked, taken aback by the unexpected gesture. "Oliver, what are you doing here?"

"Thought I'd bring a bit of spring to your doorstep." He extended the flowers toward her, their colors vibrant against the drab wooden backdrop of her home.

"Thank you, but why?" Her voice was a mix of confusion and wonder.

"Because everyone deserves to feel special, especially someone who tries so hard to hide how extraordinary they are." His sincerity hung in the cool air between them.

Lisa's fingers trembled as they reached for the bouquet, their fragrance sweet and earthy—a stark contrast to the crisp breeze.

"These are beautiful," she admitted, allowing herself a moment to admire them.

"Like I said, simple gestures." Oliver's gaze held a depth that seemed to see through her defenses.

"Simple," Lisa echoed, a smile touching her lips despite the caution still lingering in her heart.

Oliver's unwavering kindness was stirring something within her, something she wasn't sure she was ready to confront. Yet, here he was, patient and steadfast, offering her beauty without asking for anything in return.

"Come on," he said softly, gesturing down the path into town. "Let's walk together, just as friends."

"Friends," she repeated, stepping off the porch with the flowers cradled against her chest. As they started down the path, side by side, Lisa couldn't deny the excitement that fluttered in her chest, nor the warmth that spread through her at the thought of what lay ahead. Oliver Thompson had a way of making the simplest moments feel like the beginning of something thrilling.

The soft crunch of gravel beneath their feet kept a gentle rhythm as they walked, the silence between them comfortable and unforced. Lisa glanced sideways at Oliver, his profile etched against the waning light. She noted how his brow furrowed slightly with thought and how his hands found solace in the pockets of his worn jeans. His presence was reassuring and constant, like a lighthouse on a foggy night.

"Oliver," she began, her voice barely above a whisper as if testing the air for receptiveness. "I want to thank you for... this, all of this."

"Hey, there's no need." He turned to her with an easy smile that didn't quite reach his eyes. "I just want you to feel welcome here."

Lisa felt the invisible walls around her heart tremble. Welcome. It wasn't a word she'd been intimately familiar with in recent years. But the way Oliver said it, like a promise, made her entertain thoughts she'd long banished. The possibility that someone could genuinely care without ulterior motives seemed as rare as the Alaskan sun in winter. Yet, Oliver radiated that kind of warmth effortlessly.

"Sometimes I forget what that feels like," she confessed, her gaze falling to where the path unfurled before them. Each step forward was symbolic, moving toward something new and frighteningly hopeful.

"Then let's remind you," he said, his tone light but laden with meaning.

She risked another look at him and found encouragement in his steady blue eyes. Encouragement and something else—a silent vow to stand beside her through whatever storms might come. It was alarming how much she wanted to believe in that vow and lean on it.

"Tell me about your family," Lisa asked after a moment, a tentative step into the waters of her own past. She braced herself for the swell of emotions the topic usually stirred within her.

Oliver's face softened as he spoke of his parents and sister and growing up with the ocean and mountains in his backyard. His words painted pictures of community and connection, things Lisa had admired from afar but never fully grasped. As he shared stories filled with laughter and love, Lisa felt the tightness in her chest ease.

"Your turn," he nudged gently after a pause filled with the sound of waves in the distance.

"Me?" she faltered, the word catching in her throat. The emotional burden she carried felt heavy, a stark contrast to the levity of his tales.

"Only if you want to," he assured her, his voice a soothing balm.

And she did want to. For the first time in a long while, Lisa Montgomery wanted to open up and share the weight of her history with someone who might understand... with someone who cared not because they had to but because they chose to.

"Okay," she agreed, surprising even herself. "I don't know where to start."

"Start wherever you want to," Oliver said. "I've got time."

They stopped by the water's edge, where the sun's lights reflected off the gentle ripples. Lisa took a deep breath, inhaling the briny scent of the sea, and began to speak. With each word, a piece of her burden was lifted, carried away by the patient tide of Oliver Thompson's unwavering support.

Lisa spoke of her summers in her grandparents' small hometown nestled by the creek, of days spent wandering through fields painted with wildflowers, and of nights under a tapestry of stars so thick that darkness never truly fell. It was a heartwarming tale, full of innocence and wonder, but Oliver sensed the prelude of a storm lurking behind her words.

"Those summers sound magical," Oliver interjected when she paused, the warmth in his voice wrapping around her like a comforting blanket. He watched her, not just with the intent gaze of a man smitten but with an earnestness that spoke to a deeper connection.

"They were," Lisa admitted, allowing a genuine smile to curve her lips for the first time in what felt like years. "I wish my life could have stayed like that forever."

The smile faded, chased away by a cloud of sorrow. Yet, as she looked into Oliver's patient blue eyes, something within her began to thaw.

"Change can be cruel," he acknowledged, nodding slowly. His hand found a rock at their feet, tossing it into the water, where it skipped once, then twice, before succumbing to the sea. "But it can also lead us to places... to people we never expected."

"Like a fisherman with a talent for skipping stones?" Lisa quipped, the attempt at lightness betraying the tremor of vulnerability beneath.

"Exactly like that," he chuckled, his deep laugh echoing against the lull of the waves. He stepped closer, bridging the gap between them as naturally as the tide kissing the shore. "I'm here, Lisa. For whatever you want to share."

Her breath hitched, and her meticulously built guarded walls began to show cracks in his presence. The fear of judgment and pity dissipated like mist as she realized Oliver stood before her not as an adversary but as an anchor.

"Thank you, Oliver," Lisa said, her voice barely above a whisper yet laden with gratitude. "There was a time when I thought I'd never trust anyone again." The weight of her past, which she had clung to so fiercely, no longer seemed an inseparable part of her.

"Trust is earned," he replied solemnly, stepping back to give her space, yet his presence remained just as potent. "And I'm willing to take the time to earn yours."

She watched him, this man who had entered her life unexpectedly, a soothing balm to her long-festering wounds. Her heart, once barricaded, now ventured a timid beat toward hope.

"Let's walk a little longer," Lisa suggested, her tone imbued with a newfound excitement.

"Lead the way," Oliver said, gesturing forward with a gentle sweep of his arm.

A cool breeze swept across the beach as they walked side by side, weaving a path in the sand that spoke of new beginnings. Their conversation ebbed and flowed like the tide. And with every word exchanged, the seed of tender and fragile romance took root in the fertile ground of companionship, nurtured by the promise of trust and the warmth of shared confidences.

The sea whispered secrets to the shore as Oliver and Lisa walked, their footprints a testament to the path they were forging together.

"Look," Lisa said, pointing to a cluster of otters bobbing in the water. "They're holding hands to keep from drifting apart."

Oliver watched the playful creatures, then turned to see Lisa's profile outlined against the bright sun. Something about the way she observed the world, with an open-hearted wonder he'd thought lost to him, stirred a warmth in his chest more profound than he could recall.

He picked up a smooth, colorful pebble, worn by years of the ocean's caress, and offered it to her.

"For memories," he said softly.

She accepted the pebble with a smile that reached her eyes, tucking it into her pocket—a small token, yet heavy with meaning. It wasn't just a stone; it was a piece of this moment, of the steadily growing connection between them.

"Thank you, Oliver," she murmured, her voice carrying the melody of gratitude and something more profound, a note of affection that danced on the wind.

They continued along the beach, not merely side by side but together in a rhythm that felt as natural as the waves lapping at their feet.

"Have you always lived here?" Lisa asked, her curiosity about his life a sign of the walls coming down.

"Born and raised," Oliver confirmed, pride lacing his tone. "My roots run as deep as the trees. But enough about me. I feel like we've been talking only about me. What brings you joy?"

Her light and genuine laugh filled the space between them. "Well, I used to love painting," she confessed, a hint of wistfulness in her voice. "I haven't touched a brush in years, though."

"Maybe it's time you did again." His words were an encouragement, a gentle push toward reclaiming the parts of herself she'd left behind.

"Maybe," she said, and the simple word held the promise of possibility, of new chapters waiting to be written.

They soon found themselves at the edge of a quaint wooden pier. Lisa leaned against the railing, taking in the vast expanse of water.

"Lisa," Oliver began, his voice earnest, "I know we're just getting to know each other, but I want you to know that—"

"You don't have to rush," she interjected, turning to face him with a softness in her gaze. "I'm not going anywhere."

That simple assurance was enough. It became like a lighthouse guiding him through uncharted waters. They stood there, two souls, sharing a silence that spoke volumes. The bond between them was no longer just an ember of potential; it was a flame being stoked by mutual respect and the tender shoots of affection.

Chapter Five

The wind howled outside the weathered walls of Maggie's Tavern, a melody only a town like this could sing. Oliver shrugged off his heavy jacket, the salt and brine clinging to him like an old friend as he made his way to the bar. He sat on one of the stools, leather worn from years of patrons seeking refuge from the cold Alaskan air.

"Evening, Lisa," he greeted warmly, his deep voice carrying over the low hum of conversation. The bar's dim light danced in his eyes as he watched her pour another customer's drink.

"Evening, Oliver," Lisa replied without missing a beat, her hair cascading over her shoulders as she slid the glass across the polished wood. A gentle and enigmatic smile graced her lips, but it didn't reach the guarded warmth of her eyes. It had been weeks now since their walk on the beach together, and still, he didn't feel like he was getting any closer to her. It was almost as if she had pulled further away from him since that day.

"It looks like we're in for another storm tonight," Oliver observed, glancing toward the window where the frost etched intricate patterns. "The sea was churning something fierce today."

"Seems like it," Lisa responded, keeping her tone light as she wiped down the counter with practiced ease. "It'll be good for the fishing industry, though, stirring up nutrients and bringing the fish closer to the surface."

"True enough," Oliver mused, leaning back against his stool. He was the one who had taught her that. His gaze lingered on Lisa, taking in the way her hands moved with quiet efficiency, her presence a steady calm amidst the bustle of the bar. "You know, the community's grateful for the hauls we've been bringing in. Keeps the town running."

"Everyone has their part to play," Lisa said, maintaining the conversation at arm's length. She offered a soft shrug, a noncommittal gesture that seemed to encompass more than just their present exchange.

"Speaking of parts to play," Oliver ventured, a hint of curiosity threading through his words, "You've got the heart of the town in your hands every night but seem to keep to yourself during the day. What do you do in your spare time?"

Lisa met his inquiry with a polite sidestep, her smile unwavering. "Oh, I'm just a creature of habit, I suppose. And there's plenty to keep me busy around here without looking for extra trouble."

"Trouble?" Oliver chuckled softly, the sound rich and inviting. "Can't imagine someone like you stirring up much of that."

"Appearances can be deceiving," she quipped back, a flicker of something unreadable passing across her face before she turned to attend to another patron signaling for her attention.

Oliver watched her go, the mystery of Lisa Montgomery settling around him like the mist that rolled in from the sea. She was a puzzle, her pieces held tight, and though he respected the distance she put between them, he couldn't help but feel the pull to understand the depth of her tides.

Oliver leaned against the polished mahogany bar, his gaze lingering on Lisa as she expertly navigated the jovial crowd. The soft lighting cast a golden halo around her, illuminating the gentle waves of her hair. He waited for a lull in the chatter, the clinking of glasses and laughter providing a lively soundtrack to his anticipation.

"Lisa," he called out, his voice threading through the din easily. She glanced over, her hazel eyes locking with his for a fleeting moment before she approached.

"Another round, Oliver?" Her question was

routine, yet her smile held the warmth of shared familiarity.

"Actually, I was thinking," he began, the corners of his mouth curving into an earnest grin, "maybe after you're done here, we could grab a cup of coffee? There's this little place just down the road that stays open late."

The invitation hovered between them, Oliver's eyes reflecting a genuine desire for companionship. He wasn't just another patron; he was someone who noticed the subtleties of her expressions, the way her laugh seemed to carry a hint of restraint.

Lisa's smile faltered slightly, her internal walls rising instinctively at the prospect of closeness. "That's kind of you, Oliver," she replied, her tone carrying the lightest touch of regret. "But I've got some things to take care of tonight. Rain check?"

He studied her face, searching for an opening, but found only the practiced politeness she wielded like armor.

"Of course," he conceded, nodding with under-standing. "I get it—everyone needs their space."

"Thanks for understanding," she said, relief soft-ening the edges of her voice. With a graceful pivot, she returned to her duties, leaving Oliver to ponder the enigma wrapped in an apron and a captivating smile.

As the evening wore on, the bar slowly emptied. Still, the seat Oliver occupied remained filled with his patience and unwavering hope that one day, the personal space Lisa guarded so fiercely would include room for him.

Sunlight had long surrendered to the velvet of an Alaskan night by the time Oliver Thompson's boots crunched up the gravel path leading to Lisa Montgomery's modest home. Clutched in his rough, sea-worn hands was a bouquet of wildflowers—daisies and lupines, their hues a whispered secret under the moon's silver gaze. He'd plucked them from the meadows on the outskirts of town, where the earth still held the day's warmth and the air tasted of salt and pine. It had worked the last time he did this. Perhaps it would again? It was her night off; maybe she would have time for another walk. Or coffee?

The knock on the door was firm but cautious, echoing in the quiet that shrouded the house. Lisa answered, her silhouette framed by the soft glow of interior light. Surprise etched her features as she took in Oliver's unexpected presence, the bunch of flowers a stark contrast against his sturdy frame.

"Oliver?" Her voice, husky with disuse this late into the evening, carried a mixture of bewilderment and restraint. "What are you doing here?"

"Couldn't stop thinking about our chat at the bar the other night," he said, offering the flowers with a hopeful tilt of his mouth. "Figured everyone could use a bit of color in their lives."

The bouquet seemed to hover between them, a fragrant bridge attempting to span the gap that Lisa so diligently maintained. She hesitated, the shadows playing across her face as she reached out, her fingers brushing against Oliver's as she accepted the gesture. The contact was fleeting, ghost-like, leaving a trail of unspoken words lingering in the chilled air.

"Thank you, they're beautiful," she admitted, though her stance remained guarded, the door only partially ajar. "But Oliver, I really wasn't just making excuses earlier. My life... it's complicated."

"Wasn't trying to complicate things," he replied, earnestness threading through his tone like the distant call of seabirds. "Just thought you might like some flowers, is all."

Her eyes met his briefly, warmth flickering within their depths before being swiftly shuttered. "I appreciate it, truly. But... I can't." The weight of unsaid truths seemed to settle on her shoulders, a burden she bore with quiet dignity. "Please, let's keep things simple—professional."

"Understood," Oliver nodded, the edges of his smile dimming but not extinguishing. The sea had taught him patience, the slow ebb and flow of tides whispering that not all things were meant to be rushed.

"No harm in trying, though."

"Goodnight, Oliver." Lisa's voice was soft, almost lost to the rustle of the wind through the trees as she stepped back. The door closed with a gentle click that resounded like the final note of a lullaby.

He stood there for a second longer, watching the light fade from around the edges of her curtains. Then, with a sigh that mingled with the whispers of the night, Oliver turned away from the door, his heart warm with the thrill of the chase and the hope that someday, the door might open a little wider.

The briny scent of the ocean mingled with the earthy aroma of hops and barley as Oliver pushed open the door to the bar, a familiar bell chiming overhead to announce his arrival. His boots, worn from years on the deck of his fishing boat, thudded gently against the wooden floor, marking a steady rhythm akin to a heartbeat. He could feel the eyes in the room glance over him briefly—another regular returning to his haunt.

"Evening," he greeted Joe, the bartender, who offered a nod and a knowing look before turning back to polish a row of gleaming glasses. The soft hum of conversation wrapped around him like a well-worn sweater, comforting in its predictability.

Oliver made his way to a stool at the far end of the bar, one that afforded him an unobstructed view of Lisa as she navigated the tables with practiced ease. Her smile was a beacon in the dimly lit room, and her laughter, though rare, tinkled like wind chimes in a gentle breeze. He ordered a beer, the frosted mug cool to the touch, and settled in to watch the ebb and flow of patrons.

He caught snippets of her voice as she spoke with customers, each word measured and infused with kindness. The way she listened more than she talked, her head tilted ever so slightly, told a story all its own —a story of a soul preserving its secrets while serving others.

As the night wore on, Oliver found reasons to call her over, each time with a different pretext. A new napkin, a request for the evening's special, a curious inquiry about a new brew on tap. With each interaction, he offered a fragment of conversation, a thread he hoped might weave a connection between them. Yet he never tugged too hard, careful not to unravel the delicate fabric of her comfort zone.

"Are you expecting a good catch tomorrow?" Lisa asked, resting her hands on the bar in front of him. Her eyes reflected the warmth of the room but were guarded all the same.

"Sea's been generous lately," he responded, his tone light. "Hope she stays that way."

"Me too," Lisa said, her gaze drifting off toward the window where the dark silhouette of the sea pressed against the night sky. "Good for the town."

"Good for everyone," Oliver agreed, letting the conversation lull into a natural, comfortable pause. He sipped his beer, watching the condensation slide down the glass, thinking how it mirrored the slow, steady progress he was willing to make.

"Last call, folks!" Joe's voice cut through the quiet chatter, signaling the end of the night.

Patrons began to settle their tabs, donning jackets and bidding farewell. Oliver stayed put, finishing his drink as he watched Lisa begin the process of cleaning up. She moved with an efficiency that spoke of long hours and a familiarity with the task at hand.

"See you tomorrow, Lisa," he called softly as he finally stood to leave, his words tinged with hope but leaving space for her silence.

"Take care, Oliver," she replied without looking up, her voice carrying the weight of the day as she wiped down the counter.

He left a tip beneath the empty mug and made his way to the exit. The bell chimed again, a soft farewell to the day's end.

Outside, the crisp air embraced him, the stars above winking as if privy to his thoughts. Oliver let out a breath, watching it mist and disappear into the night—a testament to his presence, however fleeting.

With every visit, every casual exchange, he laid another pebble on the path leading to her world. It was a path he would tread with care, each step a silent promise to wait until the door to her life opened, not by force or sudden impulse, but by the gentle, inevitable pull of shared moments and mutual trust.

Chapter Six

Lisa was flipping through the drink orders the following night when she felt a familiar presence sidle up to the bar. Oliver's shadow fell across the polished wood, not demanding attention but simply existing in a comfortable silence that had become a staple of her evenings.

"Evening, Lisa," he greeted, his voice threading through the soft hum of conversation around them.

"Hello, Oliver," she responded, allowing herself a small smile that didn't quite reach her eyes but suggested an acknowledgment of his regularity.

"Thought I'd try something new today," he said, sliding into his usual seat. "What do you recommend?"

She pointed to a bottle behind her. "The apple cider from upstate is pretty good. Has a kick to it."

"Sounds perfect." His eyes twinkled with quiet appreciation as she poured him a glass. "You know, this reminds me of when I was a kid. We'd go apple picking every fall and make cider with my grandpa. He had this old, rickety press...."

As Oliver recounted the memory, Lisa found herself listening—not just hearing the words, but truly listening. The way he described the crispness of the apples, the laughter of his family, and the sweet scent of fresh cider painted a vivid picture that tugged at something inside her. It was rare for her to let anyone's story resonate, but there was an earnestness in Oliver's tone that made her defenses waver ever so slightly.

"Must have been nice... having those traditions," she remarked, surprised by her own contribution to the conversation.

"It was," he agreed, nodding. "But enough about me. What about you? Any childhood memories you're fond of?"

The question hung between them, an invitation she wasn't sure she wanted to accept. But something about the way he asked—without expectation or pressure—made her consider sharing a piece of herself.

"Um, well, my mom and I used to bake a lot," she started hesitantly, her hands busy tidying up the counter. She taught me how to make these amazing lemon bars. She said it was a family recipe."

"Sounds delicious," he encouraged, sensing the shift in her, the door to her past creaking open just a fraction.

"Maybe I'll bring some in some time," Lisa found

herself saying, the offer hanging in the air like a fragile promise.

Oliver's grin was gentle, appreciative, and without a hint of triumph. "I'd like that."

Their exchange was brief, the moment fleeting, yet it left a warmth lingering between them as the night wore on. As she moved along the bar, serving other patrons, Lisa caught herself stealing glances at Oliver, who seemed content to bask in the simple pleasure of their growing rapport. Each shared snippet of life, each laugh over a patron's joke, and each smile exchanged across the room wove a thread that connected them, pulling their separate worlds inch by imperceptible inch closer together.

Oliver leaned against the polished mahogany of the bar, nursing a mug of ale as he listened to Lisa recount an anecdote from her childhood. The soft glow of the overhead lanterns cast a warm light on her face, accentuating the golden flecks in her hazel eyes.

"Every summer, we'd set up a lemonade stand at the local fair," she said with a wistful smile, her voice barely rising above the hum of conversation around them. "I was probably more of a hindrance than a help back then, but Dad always said I was his best salesperson."

"Sounds like you were quite the entrepreneur,"

Oliver remarked, his gaze lingering on her face, trying to read between the lines of her story.

Lisa shrugged, a blush creeping onto her cheeks. "Hardly. I just liked counting the coins and feeling like I was part of something."

She paused, her smile fading slightly as if the memory had transported her to a place filled with both sunshine and shadows. "It was simpler back then."

"Sometimes simple is good," Oliver replied softly, aware that each shared memory was a delicate petal she plucked from the flower of her guarded heart. He sensed there were thorns hidden beneath the bloom, but he was patient, willing to wait for her to reveal them in her own time.

Their conversations had become the highlight of his evenings. With every story Lisa tentatively offered, Oliver felt the threads of connection weaving a tapestry rich with unspoken understanding. Her laughter was a melody that resonated with his own, and her silences spoke volumes he yearned to comprehend.

"Your turn," she said, nudging him gently with a challenge in her eyes. "Tell me about one of your adventures at sea."

And so, he did, recounting tales of wrestling with nets during storms, of quiet sunrises spent in solitude on the water, and the camaraderie among the crew that made the hardships bearable. His stories were infused with a passion for the sea that was as much a part of him as the salt in his veins.

As the night progressed and the bar began to empty, their conversation ebbed and flowed like the tide. They laughed over mishaps, commiserated over losses, and shared dreams that had been tucked away in the recesses of their minds. Each word spoken, each glance exchanged, seemed to draw Lisa further out of her shell, coaxing the vibrant woman hiding behind the curtain of reserve into the spotlight.

Oliver walked home that night under the starlit sky, his mind replaying their exchange, dissecting every detail. His feelings for Lisa had deepened beyond simple attraction to something richer and more complex. Yet, he was acutely aware of the barriers she had erected, the mystery that shrouded her past like the coastal fog.

He was determined to uncover the truth of what kept her so distant, not out of mere curiosity but out of a desire to understand her and perhaps share the burden she carried alone. As he reached his porch, he made a silent promise to himself and the woman slowly stealing his heart—he would be there when she was ready to reveal her dark secret, come hell or high water.

Chapter Seven

The early morning mist clung to the sleepy town like a lover's embrace as Trey Montgomery stepped off the Greyhound bus onto the gravel of Main Street. His tall frame was the first thing that caught the attention of the half-awake locals, followed by the neatly combed blond hair that seemed almost too perfect for this time of day. As he moved, his piercing green eyes swept over the storefronts and faded signs with an unsettling sharpness. There was something about him, a veneer of charm, as if each warm smile was meticulously calculated, practiced in front of mirrors until it no longer reached those cool, calculating eyes.

Oliver Thompson had been up before dawn, the sea's salt on his skin and the wind in his hair. This was his ritual, one which lent him clarity and calm before the town awakened. But the sight of the stranger unsettled him and sent ripples across the steady current of his thoughts. He watched from a distance as Trey approached Mrs. Henderson outside the bakery, his gentle inquiries at odds with the tense set of his shoulders.

"Excuse me, ma'am," Trey's voice carried, smooth like river stones, "I'm looking for someone. Maybe you've seen her?"

He produced a photograph from his phone. The phone trembled slightly in Trey's hand, betraying the nerves he tried so hard to conceal. "Her name is Lisa Montgomery," he added. "I'm Trey Montgomery."

Mrs. Henderson shook her head, but her eyes were filled with questions she didn't voice.

Oliver's gut clenched. The fisherman's senses, honed by years on the tumultuous sea, were alert. Something was amiss. The way Trey held himself, the urgency veiled behind a mask of faux-casual interest—it sang a silent alarm across Oliver's instincts. Lisa's gentle demeanor and captivating smile flashed in his mind, and with it, an overwhelming urge to protect her surged through his veins.

With every local that Trey stopped, holding out the phone with the picture of Lisa, Oliver's worry deepened. Each interaction was like a cold wave breaking against him, awakening an innate vigilance he reserved for the most treacherous storms. Oliver couldn't shake the feeling that this man, with his seemingly harmless questions and his businessman-like charm, posed a threat to Lisa's safety—a threat that Oliver could not, would not, ignore.

Oliver's heavy black leather boots crushed the small stones underfoot as he strode across the dusty road. The newcomer's back was to him, engaged in another one of his inquiries with Old Man Jensen, who squinted skeptically at Lisa's picture. Oliver's jaw clenched, a silent promise etched into the firm line of his mouth. His hands, roughened by nets and brine, curled and uncurled at his sides.

"Montgomery!" Oliver called out, his voice low but carrying. The word sliced through the crisp air, causing Trey to turn, a practiced smile gracing his lips that didn't quite reach those piercing eyes.

"Can I help you?" Trey asked, a note of false warmth in his tone as he meticulously tucked the phone away.

"Let's talk about why you're really here," Oliver stated rather than asking, his eyes not wavering from Trey's gaze.

The two men stood close, the whole of the town square holding its collective breath. A gust of wind teased the edges of Trey's coat, but he seemed unbothered by the chill, his attention solely on Oliver.

"Is this some sort of small-town welcome?" Trey quipped though the humor fell flat between them.

"Lisa's a friend," Oliver said, his voice steely yet controlled. "And friends look out for each other. So, I'll ask again—what do you want with her?"

Sensing the tension coiling like a spring, the townspeople began to form an uneven circle around them. Whispers skated on the breeze, their curiosity piqued by the standoff before them.

"Perhaps we should discuss this privately," Trey suggested coolly, his eyes narrowing ever so slightly— a hunter gauging his opponent.

"Anything you gotta say, you can say in front of everyone," Oliver countered, unwavering.

At that moment, the world seemed to shrink to the space between them. The echo of distant seabirds and the rhythm of the tide became a backdrop to their confrontation. The air grew thick with anticipation, charged with the electricity of a brewing storm.

"Very well," Trey conceded, a flash of something darker crossing his face briefly before it was masked once again by his charm. "But let's not make a scene, shall we?"

"Too late for that," Oliver muttered under his breath, aware that the eyes of the town were transfixed on the unfolding drama.

His heart hammered against his ribs—not with fear, but with a fierce determination to shield Lisa from whatever past had come calling in the form of Trey Montgomery. Oliver knew the sea like the lines on his palm and could predict a squall before it broke —but this man was an unpredictable current, and

Oliver would need all his wits to navigate the troubled waters ahead.

Oliver's boots sunk into the loose gravel as he closed the gap between him and Trey. With each step, his heart pounded harder in his chest until they were face to face, the distance between them now nothing but a breath.

"Come on. Spit it out, then," Oliver said, his voice steady as bedrock. "What do you want with Lisa?"

Trey's eyes flickered, and they lost their predatory glint for an instant. "Lisa is... she's my wife."

The words fell like a hammer blow. Of course, he had suspected this was the case when hearing the name. Yet he had hoped that he was a brother or a distant relative. Oliver felt a jarring dissonance as if the ocean itself had stood still. His jaw clenched, and he wrestled with jealousy, struggling to reconcile the image of the gentle woman who'd become part of their tight-knit community with the stranger claiming to be her spouse.

"Your wife?" Oliver repeated, his voice laced with disbelief. The very notion seemed absurd, impossible. Lisa, with her soft laughter that echoed through the docks, didn't belong to the cold world reflected in Trey's gaze.

"Look, I know how this sounds," Trey started, his

tone shifting toward something that bordered on pleading.

"Sounds?" Oliver cut him off, anger rising within him. "Sounds like you're feeding me a line of bull. Lisa never mentioned any husband." His stance was firm, arms crossed against the chill that had nothing to do with the Alaskan air.

"Would you talk about a past you wanted to run away from?" Trey countered, his voice dropping to a murmur meant only for Oliver. Something that could have been pain flickered across his face before it was smoothed away.

"Run away?" Oliver echoed, his mind racing. Lisa's quiet ways and reluctance to share her story took on new meaning in the shadow of Trey's claim.

"Look, I need to find her," Trey insisted, his posture rigid with urgency. "There are things—"

"Things she clearly doesn't want you to be a part of, or she would've stayed," Oliver interrupted, his protectiveness flaring. "You show up out of nowhere, spinning tales—why should I believe a word you say? Why should I let you anywhere near her?"

"Because I love her," Trey said simply, and it struck Oliver how those three words could hold so much weight.

"Love doesn't track someone down like prey," Oliver shot back, his blue eyes as hard as the glacial ice that ringed their town. "And it doesn't terrorize an entire community with questions."

"I'm sorry if I have come off as...," Trey's voice

cracked slightly, the mask of charm slipping. "I'm just trying to put my family back together."

"Family?" The word hung between them, fraught with complexities Oliver hadn't considered. He looked into Trey's eyes, searching for a shred of sincerity amidst the storm of doubt.

"Please," Trey said, and there was a raw edge to the word that made Oliver pause.

Oliver's heart was a battleground of suspicion and the innate desire to help—to heal. He stood motionless, the silence stretching between them, broken only by the distant call of the sea.

Trey's shoulders sagged, the lines of his face softening as if he were about to crumble beneath the weight of his turmoil.

"Please, help me. If not for me, then for the children," he whispered, each syllable laced with a palpable mix of regret and desperation. He showed him a photo of two young children, a boy and a girl. There was no doubt they were Lisa's with the way they looked just like her.

"They miss her. We all do."

Oliver's hand tightened, knuckles turning white as he fought to keep his composure. Lisa was married and had abandoned two children? It didn't seem like the Lisa he had gotten to know. The sea breeze that had always comforted him now seemed to carry the heavy burden of Trey's revelation.

"She just left one day... when I came home from work, she was just gone," Trey continued, his voice a mere echo of the confident man who had marched into town hours earlier.

Oliver wrestled with conflicting emotions crashing over him. Lisa's soft smile flashed through his mind, and he could almost hear her laughter mingling with the gulls overhead. Loyalty to her warred with a new, unsettling need to understand the truth that Trey presented—a truth that threatened to capsize everything Oliver thought he knew.

"Left her family?" Oliver echoed, his skepticism piercing through the fog of empathy that was trying to cloud his judgment. "That doesn't sound like the Lisa I know. She's... I can't believe she would do that."

Trey's eyes, those piercing mirrors to his soul, glistened with unshed tears. "You don't know the half of it. Nobody does. That's why I need to see her, talk to her, ask her why."

The fisherman felt a pang in his chest, a sympathetic ache for the pain etched so deeply into Trey's features. But still, doubt gnawed at him, a relentless tide eroding the shores of certainty. He needed more than just Trey's word; he needed solid ground to stand on.

"Please. I can't live without her. Neither can her children." Trey's outburst fractured the tense air between them. "All I have is this void where she used to be and the hope that maybe, just maybe, I can fill it again."

Oliver watched the man before him—the stranger who claimed to be Lisa's husband—and felt the sharp sting of their shared humanity. There, in the freezing cold morning air, he recognized the same helplessness that often accompanied love.

"Hope can be a cruel current," Oliver finally said, his voice barely above the whisper of the wind. "It pulls you out to sea, even when you know you should stay on land."

Trey nodded, his gaze dropping to the wooden planks beneath their feet. "I'm drowning," he murmured. "And I don't know if I'll ever find the surface again."

Oliver ran a hand through his dark hair as he exhaled slowly. The horizon was smudged with the colors of dawn, but its beauty was lost on him now. He could see the anguish etched into Trey's finely drawn features, the shadows of desperation in those green eyes that had roamed the town with an unsettling intensity.

"Alright," Oliver said, surprising himself with the decision even as it left his lips. "I know where she is."

His voice carried the weight of his resolve, tempered with a note of caution. Lisa had chosen this place to disappear, and Oliver respected her reasons

—whatever they might be. But the man before him was a tempest of sorrow, and Oliver couldn't ignore the silent plea for help—especially when it involved children.

"Really?" Trey's voice cracked with a mixture of disbelief and relief.

"Really," Oliver confirmed, though he wasn't sure which of them he was trying to convince more. Perhaps it was the fisherman's code, the unspoken rule of helping another soul adrift at sea. Or maybe it was the same protective instinct that had driven him to keep an eye on Lisa from the moment she'd set foot in their tight-knit community.

"Thank you," Trey whispered, the fight draining out of him. Oliver saw the tension in Trey's shoulders ease, but he couldn't shake the feeling that he was making a deal with the Devil or, at the very least, inviting a storm into port.

"Let's get one thing straight," Oliver said, locking eyes with Trey. "When we find her, it's her choice what happens next. I will protect her no matter what she decides. This is about making sure she's safe, nothing more."

"Understood," Trey nodded, and Oliver searched his face for any signs of the deceit he feared might lurk beneath the surface.

Oliver turned to walk away, Trey falling into step beside him. They moved through the town in silence, two men united by a woman who held both their hearts in ways they couldn't comprehend.

"Be ready for anything," Oliver warned without looking at Trey. "Finding Lisa might answer some questions, but I reckon it will raise a lot more."

Trey's only response was a quiet, troubled hum, blending with the sound of their footsteps on the cobbled street.

"But first, let me take you to the Inn. Janet will make sure you get a room, and you can put your suitcase down."

"Thank you, my friend," Trey said and placed a hand on Oliver's shoulder.

Oliver paused at the touch and closed his eyes briefly, feeling the weight of the task ahead, a boulder resting on his chest. He would never be this man's friend, no matter how hard he tried. Never.

Lisa's breath misted in the crisp Alaskan air as she took her regular morning walk, her footsteps a silent rhythm against the soft earth. The wild beauty of the landscape unfolded before her, and the towering pines and distant mountains were a comforting embrace for her introverted soul. Even after months of seeking refuge in this serene corner of the world, each morning felt like discovering a hidden treasure all over again.

As she neared the harbor, the scent of saltwater mingled with the earthy aroma of pine needles. Gulls cried above, circling the masts of fishing boats that bobbed gently on the calm waters. Lisa's eyes searched for one person in particular, and her heart fluttered when she spotted him.

Oliver stood at the edge of the dock, his figure rugged against the rising sun's backdrop. His eyes were fixed on the horizon, and even from a distance, they seemed to echo the vastness of the sea. Lisa's hand lifted in a tentative wave, and her lips parted to call out his name, eager for the warmth of his smile to brighten her day.

But the greeting froze on her tongue as another figure stepped into view, standing unnervingly close to Oliver. It was her husband, the man whose presence turned her blood to ice, the very reason she had vanished into the depths of Alaska. Panic clawed at her chest, her gentle demeanor shattering beneath the weight of fear.

Without a second thought, Lisa spun on her heel, her boots slipping slightly on the dew-kissed grass as she hurried away from the harbor. Her mind raced with the implications of their meeting. How had he found her? What did he want? Her past threatened to engulf her, but her resilience pushed her forward, propelling her back to the sanctuary of her home.

She slammed the door shut behind her, leaning against it as if to hold back the terror that nipped at her heels. With trembling fingers, Lisa dialed a number in her phone—one that promised a chance at safety.

"It's Lisa," she whispered urgently into the phone. "I need to ask you a favor."

The call was brief, a flurry of hushed words and hastily made plans. After hanging up, she grabbed a backpack from beside the door, her movements practiced and precise. She packed essentials with the efficiency of someone who knew the value of leaving no trace; her previous life had taught her how to disappear at a moment's notice.

With one last glance at the quaint cabin that had been her haven, Lisa shouldered her backpack and stepped outside. The chill of the early morning nipped at her cheeks as she set off on foot, every step away from the harbor a mix of heartache and determination. The path ahead was uncertain, but Lisa Montgomery was no stranger to forging new trails amidst the wilderness of both nature and her own heart.

Oliver's heart thrummed in his chest like the steady beat of a drum as he approached Trey, who stood outside Maggie's bar. Oliver had told him to meet him there when he knew Lisa would be in for her evening shift. He didn't want to take him to her house while still unsure about her reaction to seeing him. The late afternoon sun cast sharp shadows on the ground, carving the lines of tension that etched into Oliver's rugged features. He moved purposefully, his blue eyes reflecting the steel of the Alaskan waters he knew so well.

"Montgomery," Oliver called out, his voice firm and tinged with an edge that caused a few heads to turn from their lazy conversations on the bar's porch.

Trey turned, the sunlight glinting off his neatly combed blond hair. His eyes, usually piercing, seemed to flicker with something less certain—a hint of turmoil that belied his composed exterior.

"Thompson," he replied, the corners of his mouth twitching as if unsure whether to settle into a smile or a grimace.

The air between them grew thick with unspoken words, laden with the weight of their silent battle of wills. Oliver's stance was squared, betraying none of the protective instincts roaring within him, while Trey's posture remained relaxed, deceptively nonchalant.

"Look, I want to make sure that you know I'm not here to cause any trouble. I just want to see her again and hopefully talk to her," Trey said after a moment, his voice cracking with an unexpected rawness. The façade of control slipped, revealing a glimpse of the man driven by love and fear.

"I understand that, but we also have to respect the fact that she came here for a reason, and she didn't tell you where she went for a reason, and that's her choice," Oliver insisted, his instinct to protect overpowering the doubts swirling in his mind. He needed answers and would get them—one way or another.

"Because if you're here to cause her any more pain—" Oliver left the threat hanging in the air.

Trey's shoulders sagged slightly, a sigh escaping him, giving life to his vulnerability.

"She's my wife, damn it. And she is here when her children are crying for her at home. All I want is to be with her through whatever comes. I love her, and I need her to know that."

Silence fell over them with the exception of the distant cry of seagulls and the soft lap of waves against the shore—two men bound together by their love for the same woman, each driven by very different demons.

"Help me, Thompson," Trey pleaded, his eyes shimmering once again with unshed tears. "Please."

Oliver's resolve wavered, his emotions a tempest as fierce as any he'd faced at sea. But the thought of Lisa, her soft smile and quiet strength, guided his next words.

"Alright. We do this together but we do it right —for Lisa. Her shift is starting now. She should be in here, but remember, if she doesn't want to talk to you"

Trey raised his hands. "Then I will back off. Naturally. You can trust me."

Oliver led the way inside the tavern. The door swung open to a chorus of greetings and laughter—a melody that had always been the heartbeat of the community.

Inside, the air was rich with the scent of fried fish and spilled beer, a comforting reminder of simpler times.

Maggie spotted them first, her red curls bouncing as she made her way over. Her eyes flickered between Oliver and Trey, and a question formed on her lips before she could speak.

"Have you seen Lisa?" Oliver cut straight to the chase, his eyes reflecting a mix of hope and concern.

"Lisa? No, she hasn't come in today. As a matter of fact, she was supposed to be here an hour ago. I haven't seen her since yesterday," Maggie replied, wiping her hands on her apron. "Come to think of it, yesterday she seemed... preoccupied. Is everything okay?"

"Long story," Trey interjected, his voice betraying a hint of impatience. "We need to find her."

"Alright, I'll try and call her," Maggie said, grabbing her cell phone. She pressed the button and placed it against her ear, a concerned look on her face. She looked at them both, then shook her head. "It's going straight to voicemail. Maybe try and go to her house? Meanwhile, I'll ask around," Maggie assured them, her maternal instincts kicking in as she surveyed Trey with a cautious eye. "Let's not panic until there's reason to."

"Thank you," Oliver said, offering a grateful smile that didn't quite reach his eyes. He was worried now.

As they moved through the crowded room, the patrons' chatter seemed to swell around them, filling the space with an undercurrent of intrigue. Sarah caught Oliver's arm, her freckled face etched with worry.

"Oliver, what's going on? People are talking." Her voice was almost lost in the din, but her earnestness was unmistakable.

"Nothing to be concerned about, just looking for Lisa," he replied, maintaining a calm he didn't feel. "Keep an eye out for her, will you?"

"Of course!" Sarah bounced on the balls of her feet, eager to help.

Exiting the warmth of the bar into the cool embrace of the twilight, Oliver took a deep breath, tasting the salt on the breeze. Trey stood beside him, a statue of tension and resolve.

"Next, we try her house," Oliver suggested. "Maybe she's still there."

"Let's hope so," Trey murmured, and there was a softness to his words that surprised Oliver, a fleeting glimpse of the man Lisa had married.

Together, they strode down the lantern-lit streets, the echo of their footsteps a rhythmic drumbeat against the cobblestones. Their shared mission brought an unexpected camaraderie, a bond forged by necessity and a mutual desire to ensure Lisa's safety.

They reached the cabin she had rented and knocked, but the windows were dark, and the silence within was speaking volumes. Lisa wasn't there.

Oliver was beginning to get nervous. The mystery of her disappearance hung heavy in the air, a puzzle with pieces scattered by fate and circumstance.

Chapter Eight

Oliver's boots crunched on the frosted underbrush as he hastened his pace, the chilling Alaskan air biting at his cheeks. It was dark night now, and he could barely see the starry sky over the towering pines surrounding him. His breath hung in puffs of white vapor, each exhale a testament to the urgency that propelled him forward through the wilderness, guided by only his flashlight.

He had left the town behind in a flurry after receiving a tip from Joe, the grizzled barkeep who knew everyone and everything that happened in their small community. Joe told him that Lisa had called him earlier in the day and asked if she could borrow his cabin in the woods for a few days. Joe had told her about the cabin and how he enjoyed going there in the summers to get some peace and tranquility as it was completely hidden from the main roads. Joe said she had sounded in distress and that he was concerned for her safety, and that's why he told Oliver so he could go check on her.

Oliver had chosen not to tell Trey. He needed to talk to Lisa by himself first. He needed to know what was going on.

The cabin came into view, an isolated haven nestled between the embrace of aged cedars. A wisp of smoke curled from the chimney, indicating that Lisa was awake, perhaps unable to sleep. He approached the door and knocked, his backpack tight on his shoulders, but no one opened it. He grabbed the door handle, but the door was locked. Then he knocked again—this time harder.

"Lisa!" His voice cut through the silence of the woods.

"Oliver? Is that you?"

Relieved to hear her voice, he calmed down. "Yes, Lisa. Let me in."

"Are you alone?"

"Yes," he said. "It's just me here. Please, open the door."

The lock clicked, and the door slid open. There she was. Her gorgeous face and beautiful eyes stared up at him, again stealing his heart. Her eyes, usually warm and inviting, widened with a mix of surprise and alarm.

"Oliver, what are you doing here?"

"Sorry for barging in like this," Oliver interjected,

stepping inside and sweeping the room with a quick glance. "But I was worried."

His gaze locked onto hers, deep blue eyes conveying a seriousness that made her heart hitch. She straightened up, brushing ash from her hands, her gentle demeanor giving way to a sharpened attentiveness.

"Worried?" she asked, her voice steady despite the fear that crept into her eyes.

"Yeah," Oliver confirmed, moving closer. "You disappeared without a word. What happened?"

"Nothing," she said. "I'm just... I decided to take a few days off. Joe let me borrow this cabin; it was really nice of him...."

Oliver grabbed her arm. He looked deep into her eyes. "Tell me the truth. What's going on, Lisa?"

She sighed, and tears welled into her eyes. "I'm in trouble."

The gravity of her words seemed to settle over the cabin, cloaking the room in a palpable tension. Lisa's pulse quickened, yet there was a resilience in her stance, a testament to the trials she had already overcome.

"Because of your ex-husband?" Oliver asked. "Trey?"

She paused and seemed to shiver. "I can't... Oliver, I don't know what to say... how to explain it. I can't talk about it. But he can't find me, do you hear?"

"Okay," he breathed out, nodding slowly. "But he will sooner or later. People in town talk, and someone might already have told him where to find you. I know he talked to Sheriff Coleman and reported you missing, which means they're looking for you."

"He can't find me. Do you hear me, Oliver? He simply can't."

Oliver watched a flicker of resolve light up her expression, and despite the perilous situation, he couldn't help but feel a surge of admiration for the woman before him.

"Let's figure this out together," he said, offering her a small, reassuring smile that belied the racing of his own heart. She didn't need to tell him more. He knew by the look on her face that he had to help her. "We'll have to leave," he said.

Lisa returned the smile, albeit a strained one, and in that shared moment, a silent pact was made. Oliver felt a renewed sense of purpose radiate from within, fueled by the bond that had quietly woven itself between them amid the chaos of their shared plight. It was heartwarming, even in the face of danger, and he knew they were ready to face whatever lay ahead, side by side.

Oliver's hand moved to Lisa's shoulder, a comforting weight as he spoke with quiet urgency. "We need to pack up now and leave nothing behind."

Lisa's fingers curled into the fabric of her shirt, a visible tremor betraying her anxiety. The thought of fleeing again gnawed at her insides, a relentless reminder of a life turned fugitive.

"Oliver," she whispered, her voice a fragile thread, "I'm scared."

He stepped closer, his presence a solid reassurance in the dimly lit room. In his gaze was an unspoken promise, a stronghold amidst the storm.

"I know it's hard, Lisa, but I won't let anything happen to you. Trust me, I've got your back. We'll leave tomorrow at first light. Let me help you." He reached out, his rough fisherman's hands gentle as they folded over hers.

Her eyes met his, searching for the conviction behind his words. Something about Oliver, something steadfast and true, anchored her amidst the chaos. A softness played across his features, the kind that only wilderness and weather can carve, and she felt a flicker of hope.

"Okay," Lisa said, her decision firming with the resolve reflected in his supportive gaze. "Let's do this together."

A spark of excitement mingled with the fear, igniting a warmth that spread through her chest. With Oliver by her side, the perils of the unknown seemed less daunting. They were two hearts beating against the odds, ready to face the wilds beyond their temporary haven.

He slept on the couch till the morning broke and sunshine filled the cabin. She was already awake, packing her few belongings. Oliver's hands moved deftly, swinging his backpack onto his back, the fabric worn from years of braving the elements. Lisa followed suit, her fingers trembling slightly as she folded her clothes with practiced precision, each fold a silent mantra for safety. The cabin, once a sanctuary bathed in soft lamplight and shadow, transformed back into an empty shell with every item she tucked away.

"Make sure we leave no trace of you behind," he said.

Lisa nodded, her eyes scanning the bedroom. She plucked a single hair from the pillow, a strand that glinted like spun copper against the rough fabric. Her existence here, now reduced to whispers and echoes, was being erased with meticulous care.

"Ready?" His voice was low, tinged with the urgency of their predicament.

She met his gaze, her own reflecting a blend of resolve and vulnerability. "As I'll ever be."

Stepping outside and heading toward Oliver's car, Lisa paused. Oliver came up behind her and immediately saw what she did: three cars approaching on the previously empty dusty road. Two were from the sheriff's office, and Trey Montgomery drove the last one.

"He's coming. He'll have the police on his side. He might even have told them that you kidnapped me or that I'm in trouble, and you're the cause of it. There's no telling what he told them to get them on his side," Lisa said.

She gasped fearfully and pulled back. Seeing this, Oliver grabbed her hand in his and pulled.

"Come. We'll go out the back. I know these woods and the mountains very well. We can disappear in there. I can lead us through without being seen."

He pulled her hand, and she shook off the state of shock she had been in. The crisp air greeted them with the sharp tang of pine and earth as they stepped out on the back porch. The world beyond the cabin was vast, an open canvas of green and brown hues waiting to envelop them in its untamed embrace. It was beautiful and scary at the same time. Oliver led the way, his steps sure and silent on the needle-strewn ground.

They made for the mountains, nature's fortresses that loomed in the distance, promising refuge in their secluded crevices. Each step further from the cabin was a step deeper into the unknown, but Lisa felt the stirrings of anxiety within her—a beating heart thumping in her chest at the thought of them being found.

Oliver guided her through dense underbrush and over jagged rocks. He knew these paths like the lines on his sunbaked hands, each turn and incline imprinted from childhood explorations. His assurance was a guiding light piercing the uncertainty shrouding Lisa's heart.

His hand found hers, their fingers intertwining naturally. The warmth of his touch seeped into her skin, a silent vow that bolstered her courage. Together, they climbed higher, where the sky stretched wide, the air thinned, and the promise of safety nestled among the peaks of their mountain haven.

Oliver's laughter, a rich baritone, cut through the rustle of leaves and the occasional snap of a twig underfoot. Lisa glanced up at him, her breaths coming in short puffs as they ascended the incline.

"You're telling me you actually convinced your entire class that moose could tap dance if you sang to them?"

"Swear on my granddad's fishing boat," he said with a mischievous glint in his eyes. His stories were like stepping stones across a river, each one a distraction from the churning current of fear below.

Lisa couldn't help but chuckle despite the gravity of their situation. Oliver's reminiscences had an infectious joy, a boyish charm that hadn't been dimmed by time or hardship. She watched his shoulders rise and fall with his gait, strong and steady, as he recounted tales of youthful escapades among these very mountains that now shielded them.

"Once, during the winter solstice," Oliver began another tale, his voice softening with the reverence of a cherished memory, "my friends and I stayed up all night just to see the first light break over Eagle Crest. It was like the whole world woke up with us."

The image settled into Lisa's mind, painting a serene picture vastly different from the life she knew. She felt her own guarded walls begin to crumble, inspired by Oliver's vulnerability.

"My hometown never had mountains," she shared, her words tumbling out hesitantly. "Just endless fields of corn that seemed to touch the sky. We'd run through them, pretending we were explorers discovering new worlds."

Oliver's smile was gentle and encouraging. He squeezed her hand as they walked, a silent invitation to keep going—through the terrain and her own history. The trust between them was fragile, yet it grew with each step and shared story.

"Those fields sound beautiful," he said, his voice wrapping around her like a warm blanket. "But I bet they didn't have views like this."

He gestured toward a clearing where the mountainside fell away to reveal the valley below. The sight stole Lisa's breath; it was a tapestry of greens and golds woven seamlessly under the vast expanse of the sky. For a moment, her fears evaporated, leaving only wonder.

"Thank you, Oliver," she whispered, not just for

the view but for the feeling of being seen and heard, maybe even understood.

"Thank you for trusting me," he replied, his smile reaching his eyes.

Together, they stood on the precipice of the world, their hearts lighter than they'd been in days. Oliver's childhood stories and Lisa's glimpse into her own past wove a bond of love and comfort amidst the wilderness. This journey was fraught with peril, but it was also an unexpected adventure, one they would navigate side by side.

The fading light of dusk painted the horizon in strokes of magenta and orange as Oliver led Lisa to a hidden dell, canopied by ancient pines. Their needles whispered secrets to the wind, offering a sense of seclusion and protection. Here, they would make their camp for the night.

"Perfect," Oliver murmured, setting down his backpack with care.

Lisa followed suit, her eyes scanning the small clearing that seemed to embrace them with its tranquil presence.

"Never thought I'd be so grateful for all those camping trips with my dad," Lisa said, managing a smile as she assisted Oliver in gathering an assortment of fallen branches and stones.

"Same here," Oliver chuckled. "Dad had me build fires before I could even tie my own shoes."

His hands moved with practiced ease, arranging the wood in a precise formation while Lisa collected dry leaves and twigs for kindling.

With a lighter, sparks leaped into existence, hungry for fuel. They coaxed a flame to life, nurturing it until it crackled assertively, banishing the encroaching chill of the Alaskan twilight.

Satisfied with their handiwork, they sat back on the mossy ground, the fire's glow painting their faces with flickering shades of warmth. The forest around them seemed to hold its breath, respecting their sanctuary.

"This is nice," Lisa sighed, drawing her knees up to her chest and wrapping her arms around them. "Scary, but... nice."

Oliver nodded, throwing another log onto the fire. "We're safe here, Lisa. For tonight, at least."

They spoke of dreams—Oliver's humble desire to keep his father's fishing business afloat amidst modern challenges and Lisa's yearning to start a small business without the shadow of her past looming over her.

"Sometimes, I dream of a little café by the sea, windows open to catch the salt breeze, while the smell of baked goods fills my nostrils inside," Lisa confessed, her voice threaded with longing as she stared into the dancing flames.

"Sounds peaceful," Oliver replied, his blue eyes

reflecting the firelight. "You'll have it one day. I'm sure of it."

Fears crept into their dialogue next, the sort that clung stubbornly to one's soul.

"I fear letting you down more than anything," he admitted, his tone earnest, the lines of his face etched with determination. "But I won't. We've got each other's backs, Lisa. I got you."

Their connection deepened, roots intertwining in the fertile soil of shared vulnerability. Laughter mingled with solemn promises, the kind forged in the crucible of adversity.

As the night drew its curtain tighter around them and the stars began their silent vigil overhead, Oliver and Lisa found comfort not only in the fire's warmth but in one another's presence—a light of hope in their uncertain journey.

Oliver stood from where they had been sitting, brushing off the dirt from his pants, and disappeared into the blanket of darkness that surrounded their makeshift camp. Lisa watched him go, her gaze lingering on the place where his silhouette merged with the night. The fire crackled and spat, a comfortable soundtrack to her thoughts as she wrapped her arms around her knees.

Minutes later, Oliver reemerged into the circle of light cast by the fire, his hands behind his back and a mischievous glint in his eyes. In the quiet of the Alaskan wilderness, even the smallest gestures seemed amplified, carrying a gravity that was both heartwarming and exciting.

"Close your eyes," he said, a playful tone dancing in his voice.

Lisa raised an eyebrow but complied, the corners of her mouth tilting upward in anticipation. She heard the rustle of leaves and felt the warmth of his presence as he knelt before her.

"Okay, open them."

When she did, her eyes met the sight of a small bouquet of wildflowers, their petals a delicate contrast against Oliver's rough hands. They were a splash of color in the dimness, tiny beacons of resilience that had pushed through the earth to reach for the sky.

"For you," he said, his voice softer now.

The flowers brought an unbidden smile to her face, warming her cheeks more than the flames ever could. She reached out, her fingers brushing his as she took the offering. The blooms were simple yet stunning—a vibrant reminder of life's persistent beauty amidst the chaos.

"Thank you, Oliver," Lisa whispered, her voice laced with genuine affection.

"Every time we see these flowers, we'll remember this night," he replied, "the night we didn't just survive, we lived."

The stars hung above like a tapestry of diamonds,

each a silent sentinel witnessing the unfolding chapter of their lives.

In the vast silence, with only the whisper of the wind accompanying them, Oliver reached for Lisa's hand. Their fingers entwined naturally as if molded from the same clay, and for a moment, the weight of their circumstances lifted, leaving only the purity of human connection.

With their hands clasped together, they gazed upward, lost in the cosmic dance of light that played across the heavens. Each star seemed to twinkle with approval, blessing the bond that had formed between two kindred spirits fighting against the odds.

"Look at that," Oliver pointed toward the constellation that mirrored the wildflowers in Lisa's grasp, "even the stars are blooming tonight."

And there, under the watchful eyes of the universe, they shared a tender moment, a gentle reprieve from the relentless pursuit that had driven them deep into the heart of Alaska. Everything else faded away as their breath mingled in the chilly air, and their eyes locked in silent conversation. There was just Oliver and Lisa, the wildflowers, and the boundless sky—a moment of perfect tranquility in a world that seldom offered such gifts.

The warmth of the fire crackled between them, casting dancing shadows on their faces as they huddled close for warmth in the brisk mountain air. Lisa shifted slightly, her gaze lingering on the embers before finding Oliver's steady, reassuring blue eyes.

"Oliver," she began, her voice barely rising above the murmur of the wilderness around them, "I can't thank you enough." She brushed a stray lock of hair from her face, her eyes reflecting the flames and something deeper—an amalgam of fear, relief, and burgeoning hope. "For everything you've done... for being here."

Oliver's hand was steady as he reached out, gently squeezing her shoulder; his touch conveyed a silent promise of solidarity. His presence was an anchor in the chaotic storm that had become her life.

"Lisa, there's no need to thank me. I told you when we started this—I'm with you through thick and thin. You don't even have to explain why we're running. I trust you."

She nodded, swallowing back the lump of emotion that threatened to choke her words.

"But you didn't have to risk so much. You've been..." Lisa paused, searching for the right words, "... my strength when I felt I had none left."

He smiled softly at her, the corners of his eyes crinkling in a way that made her heart flutter despite the cold and fear. "That's what people do for each other, Lisa. We're stronger together than we are apart."

"Even when 'together' means being fugitives?" Her question had a hint of bitterness but was tempered by the undeniable comfort she found in his unwavering conviction.

"Especially then." His voice was firm, resolute. He leaned forward, his hands animated as he spoke, projecting confidence that seemed almost tangible in the dim light. "No matter what comes our way, I'll do whatever it takes to keep you safe. I'm not going anywhere."

His sincerity was unmistakable, and for a moment, it insulated her from the chill of the night and the uncertainty of their situation. In Oliver, she found an unexpected sanctuary, a protective shield made not of armor but of empathy, resolve, and quiet courage.

"Thank you," Lisa said again, this time allowing a small, heartfelt smile to grace her lips. "For standing by me."

"Always," he replied, his tone laced with an unspoken vow.

They sat in silence then, letting the conversation fade into the sounds of the forest and the soft crackle of the fire. Above them, the stars continued their watch, and below, two souls drew strength from each other, their bond solidifying with every shared heartbeat. Oliver's promise hung in the air, a steadfast oath in an ever-shifting landscape, his commitment as constant as the northern star that guided them through the darkness.

～

The embers of the dying fire cast a warm glow over their makeshift camp, flickering shadows dancing across the bowed walls of their shelter. Lisa nestled closer to Oliver, her head resting against the steady beat of his heart. The rhythm was a soothing counterpoint to the symphony of nocturnal sounds surrounding them—the hoot of an owl, the whisper of leaves, and the distant murmur of a creek.

Oliver's arms tightened around her, one hand stroking the curve of her shoulder in gentle reassurance. His warmth seeped into her bones, a balm to the chill of the mountain air. In the cocoon of his embrace, the weight of their plight seemed to lift just enough for breath to come easier, for the tightness in her chest to unfurl.

"Better?" he murmured, his breath ruffling through her hair.

"Much," she whispered back, her voice barely audible above the crackling remnants of the fire.

They lay there, two fugitives from fate, wrapped in a blanket that smelled like pine needles and earth. The fabric was rough against her skin, but it was welcome, a tangible reminder of the reality they faced together. She felt his lips press a soft kiss atop her head—affirming their silent pledge to each other.

The constellations above played hide and seek with the clouds, painting pictures of hope on the infinite canvas of night. Lisa found herself tracing the lines of Ursa Major, the Great Bear, drawing strength from its eternal presence. How many others had looked up at these same stars, seeking solace in their unchanging light?

"Look," Oliver said suddenly, his voice tinged with wonder.

Lisa followed his gaze, catching sight of a shooting star streaking across the sky, a fleeting spark in the vast darkness.

"Make a wish," he encouraged softly, his fingers interlacing with hers.

She closed her eyes, summoning a wish from the depths of her longing—a wish for safety, peace, and the promise of days spent free from fear. And maybe, just maybe, a future where this man beside her could be more than just a protector but a partner in every sense.

"Done," she said, opening her eyes to meet his gaze. They shared a smile, an unspoken acknowledgment of their shared dreams and the fragile hope that sustained them.

Gradually, the world beyond their shelter receded, leaving only the intimacy of their entwined forms. Oliver's steady breathing became a lullaby, lulling her toward sleep. As her consciousness waned, she clung to the feeling of his arms around her, of the steadfast beat of his heart against her cheek.

In the quiet before sleep claimed her, Lisa allowed herself to believe in the possibility of a tomorrow where fear didn't dictate their lives. For now, though, she had this moment—this perfect, peaceful moment—and the man whose embrace promised a safe haven amidst the storm.

They drifted off, the challenges of the journey ahead eclipsed by the serenity of their shared warmth. Here, under the watchful eyes of the stars, they found refuge in each other, their slumber a testament to the human capacity for hope in the face of adversity. Oliver and Lisa, against the odds, were asleep and united, embarking on a perilous path not alone but together, their hearts beating as one in the silence of the Alaskan wilderness.

Chapter Nine

The door of the Rusty Anchor swung open with a gust that mingled the brisk air with the warmth of spiced rum and laughter. Oliver Thompson's sea-storm eyes swept across the dimly lit interior, flickering over worn wooden tables until they anchored on the corner booth where Mark and Sarah sat, shoulders hunched in conversation. Oliver had asked them to meet him there, in a pub far outside their hometown, where no one would know him, and not to tell anyone where they were going. He needed their help.

"Hey, Ollie!" Sarah's voice chirped above the tavern's hum as she spotted him.

"Hello," Oliver grunted, moving past clusters of patrons with a nod. As he approached his friends, the weight of the situation pressed down on him like a wave ready to break.

"Mark, Sarah, I need your help," Oliver said,

urgency sharpening his usually calm baritone. He dropped into the seat opposite them, muscles tense beneath his thick fisherman's sweater. The joviality that often accompanied their meetings was absent, replaced by a raw, palpable concern that drew a line between this visit and countless others.

"What's going on?" Mark's deep voice rumbled, his bear-like stature rigid with alertness. The light caught the glint of his shaved head, and his hand paused mid-gesture, beer halfway to his lips.

"It's Lisa," Oliver began, leaning in so that only the two of them could hear. "Her husband is looking for her. He's not right. She's scared, and I can't just stand by. We've got to do something—fast."

Sarah's freckles seemed to stand out more starkly against her suddenly pale skin, her vivacious spirit momentarily overshadowed by the gravity of Oliver's words.

"They've been coming to the bar and asking questions about her...." Her voice trailed off. "I had a feeling something was up. Is she okay?"

"For now, yes," Oliver affirmed, nodding solemnly.

"But the police are involved," Mark said. "Are you sure she is telling the truth?"

Oliver nodded again. "She's not one to make things up or overreact. That's why I'm worried."

"You haven't known her for very long," Mark said.

"I know when someone is afraid," Oliver said. "And she is very, very scared."

"Say no more, Ollie," Sarah interjected, a firm resolve settling over her features. You're talking about our Lisa. Whatever you need, consider it done."

"Thank you," Oliver exhaled, the tension in his shoulders ebbing slightly with their quick show of solidarity. "We've got to keep her safe, and I think I know where to start. But we have to move quickly."

"Lead the way," Sarah piped up, her usual spark reigniting with a fierce protectiveness. "Lisa's my girl. No one messes with one of our own."

Mark's hand found its way to the wooden grain of the table, fingers drumming a silent beat. Sarah mirrored his worry with a tight press of her lips, the freckles on her cheeks stark against her pallor. They locked eyes, a silent conversation passing between them before turning to face Oliver, their expressions hardened into resolve.

"Lisa's got us," Mark finally said, his voice low and steady. "Whatever it is—digging through hell or high water—we're in."

Sarah's nod was vehement, her short black hair catching the light as she moved. "We can't just sit around while someone hurts one of our own," she added, her usually vibrant tone edged with steel.

Oliver's eyes reflected the bar's dim lighting, gratitude flickering within their depths. He leaned forward, elbows on the table, drawing them both into the circle of his urgency.

"I've been thinking," he began, his voice a conspiratorial whisper.

"Are you suggesting we do some digging?" Sarah asked, her curiosity piqued.

"Exactly." Oliver's gaze didn't waver. "You guys are good with computers and stuff. You know I'm terrible at that kind of thing. Give me the great outdoors, and I can help you survive for months, but give me a computer, and I'm completely lost. So that's why I need you two. If we can find anything about Trey Montgomery, maybe we can protect Lisa. She won't talk about him, but I need to know. Who is this guy?"

Mark rubbed his beard, thoughtful. "There's bound to be something."

"Then, it's settled. We'll start piecing together Trey's history," Oliver decided, his determination infectious. "It's time we understand the monster lurking behind that charm."

"What if he isn't a monster?" Mark said pensively.

"What do you mean?" Oliver asked.

"We don't know his reasons for coming here," he added.

"Listen, I know that Lisa is afraid; I see it in her eyes every time his name comes up. That's all I need to know that this man isn't right. Why else would she run from him?"

"Okay, okay," Mark said. "Just playing the devil's advocate here. I'm with you. All the way."

Oliver glanced between his two loyal friends, a surge of gratitude warming his chest despite the chill that still clung to his jacket. With allies like Sarah and Mark, he felt a renewed confidence that, together, they could shield Lisa from the storm brewing around her.

"Sarah and I will check for public records—court filings, police reports, anything that stands out," Mark said, his broad shoulders squared in determination. He had gone to his car to get his laptop and set it up on the table between them. Oliver sighed, grateful for his friends and their support in this. He didn't know where else to go. He had to help Lisa somehow. He just knew it in his heart.

"Do we know which state or maybe town they came from?" Mark asked. "Where did they live?"

"In the Seattle area," he said. "That's all Lisa would tell me. She doesn't know I'm talking to you guys; she would be mad if she knew. I told her I was going to get some supplies. We've been staying at an abandoned cabin on the other side of the mountain. She's there now, waiting for me. I promised I would bring her chocolate and some Chardonnay. I can't be gone too long, or she'll get worried."

"We'll hurry," Mark said.

"Let me try," Sarah said and pulled the laptop closer.

"Hey," Mark said.

"Oh, what are you complaining about?" she said with a mischievous grin. "You know I'm faster and way better at this sort of stuff than you."

Mark scoffed.

"She's got a point," Oliver said.

"I guess so," Mark added, still slightly offended.

Sarah's freckles seemed to merge into a single blush of focus as her eyes darted across the computer screen, searching databases with Mark leaning in beside her, offering quiet suggestions whenever she hesitated.

As the minutes ticked away, each scrap of information, every turned page and clicked link, brought them closer to understanding the man who had ensnared Lisa. There was no room for error, no time for second-guessing. They were a trio bound by concern, driven by the need to protect one of their own, their unity a testament to the strength of small-town ties.

Oliver's pulse thrummed in his ears, not just from the adrenaline of the hunt but also from the realization of what was at stake. They were racing against more than just time; they were racing against Trey's next move.

Oliver's hands stilled, his breath hitching as he stared at the words on his phone screen. A chill crept up his spine. There, nestled between a story about a local pie contest and an announcement for the annual fishing derby, was a headline that made his heart drop:

Domestic Dispute Ends in Hospitalization.

His eyes quickly scanned the article, absorbing every detail with growing alarm. The woman's name was different, but the perpetrator was unmistakably Trey Montgomery. Descriptions of his volatile outburst painted a picture far removed from the charismatic facade he presented to the world. Oliver's jaw clenched; this was the hidden truth behind Trey's smile. The woman had ended up in the hospital with broken bones and a severe concussion. That had to be why Lisa was scared—why she had run.

Across the wooden table, Sarah was hunched over the computer, her fingers typing with surprising grace. Mark leaned close, pointing at the screen with a determination that belied his usually carefree demeanor. They were a study in contrast—her lithe figure next to his brawny frame—but united in their purpose.

"Got something else," Sarah whispered, her voice barely rising above the sound of the keyboard. She tapped the screen where a digital copy of a police report filled the display. It detailed an altercation in a neighboring town to where the first report had been from, complete with statements that echoed the aggression Oliver had just read about. The final line stated that the victim had been granted a restraining order against Trey Montgomery, and the victim had been his girlfriend at the time.

"Send me a copy of that one as well," Oliver said.

Mark met Sarah's gaze, the usual mirth in his eyes replaced by a steely resolve. He gave a subtle nod, an unspoken pact between them that they would see this through for Lisa's sake. Oliver felt a surge of gratitude for his friends' unwavering support, as much as he felt the weight of responsibility tighten around his shoulders.

They were in this together—a fisherman, a waitress, and a lumberjack—each bringing their own strengths to a fight that had become personal. Their small-town roots ran deep, their loyalty to one another unshakable. And now, armed with the truth, they were ready to protect one of their own from the storm that was Trey Montgomery.

Oliver's hands sifted through the compiled evidence, his fingers tapping on the screen of his phone, skimming through the police reports and newspaper clippings once more. Across from him, Sarah's pen danced across a fresh notepad, bullet-pointing key facts that could not, should not, be overlooked.

"Once this is all in order," Oliver said, breaking

the silence that had cocooned them, "we take it straight to the sheriff."

"Will he listen?" Sarah asked, worry creasing her brow as she capped her pen.

"He has to," Mark grumbled, his voice a low rumble of certainty. "We've got enough here to paint Trey as the bad guy he truly is."

"Then let's hope the law is on Lisa's side," Oliver replied, a surge of adrenaline bolstering his spirit.

Oliver stood tall, his gaze locked with Mark and Sarah's. A silent commitment passed between them, a fiery fusion of camaraderie and conviction.

"Ready?" he asked, though it was less of a question and more of a battle cry.

"Let's do this," Sarah affirmed, a spark igniting in her eyes.

"Lead the way, Captain," Mark offered with a half-smile that belied the gravity of their mission.

They exited the pub, the hushed atmosphere of knowledge and wisdom giving way to the crisp air of impending action. The trio moved with purpose, their steps synchronized on the sun-dappled path. Oliver's pulse quickened, not with fear, but with the thrill of the chase, the chance to right a wrong, to be the shield for someone who had weathered far too many storms alone.

Oliver felt it in his bones, the warmth of friendship and the heat of determination melding within him. They were no longer just three individuals; they were a united front, ready to face whatever lay ahead.

And with that unity came strength, hope, and the very essence of what made their small town more than just a dot on the map—it was home, and they would go to the ends of the earth to keep it safe, especially for one of their own.

Chapter Ten

The old cabin was a rustic hideaway, nestled among the whispering pines like a well-kept secret. Lisa peered out the window, her breath fogging up the glass as she saw him approach. He had been gone all day, and she had been so worried. Finally, he was back, carrying a bag of groceries.

Oliver's sturdy fisherman's boots were thudding against the wooden steps as he ascended the porch. Lisa opened the door with a relieved gasp. "Are you okay? Did anyone see you or follow you?"

"No, we're fine. I found a small market a few miles away and got what we needed. Some bread, some chocolate and of course some wine. There's no saying if it's any good, but hey, it's wine, right?"

She smiled and opened the door for him to enter the cabin.

The last ray of sunlight dipped behind the horizon, and the cabin once again became their cloistered haven, fortified against the encroaching night—and Trey.

Lisa's gaze lingered on Oliver, taking in his rugged profile silhouetted against the dimming light. She felt a surge of gratitude for the man who had become her protector, her confidant.

"Oliver," Lisa began, her voice barely above a whisper yet laden with emotion. "I don't know how to thank you. You're so good to me—more than anyone ever has been." Her hazel eyes shimmered with unshed tears, reflecting the earnestness of her words.

Oliver stepped closer, his presence enveloping her in a warmth that had nothing to do with the cabin's shelter.

"Lisa, there's no need to thank me," he said, his tone gentle but firm. "I couldn't stand by and watch when you were afraid—not when I could do something about it. I don't know what has happened to you, but I believe you and trust you."

Her heart swelled at his kindness, the rough edges of his fisherman's hands now tender as they cupped her face. It was an act so full of care that it breached the walls she'd built around herself. For a moment, the world outside—with its threats and fears—melted away, leaving only the two of them, connected by a bond that had been strengthened through adversity.

"Oliver, being here with you feels like... like

coming home," she confessed, allowing her hands to rest against his chest.

He smiled then, a smile that reached his eyes and seemed to light up the room with its sincerity.

"Then let's make sure we keep this home safe—for both of us."

Lisa knew that whatever lay ahead, they would face it together. And in that moment, her gratitude morphed into something deeper, a thread of emotion that wove itself tightly around her heart.

With the evening chill beginning to seep through the cabin walls, Oliver knelt before the fireplace. His hands, so adept at navigating the treacherous waters off the Alaskan coast, now worked to bring warmth to their sanctuary. Lisa watched as he stacked the kindling in a precise geometry, a foundation for the logs that would soon take flame. The strike of a match, the whisper of fire catching—it was a moment's alchemy that turned simple wood into a source of life.

"Got it," Oliver murmured, satisfaction coloring his voice as the fire caught hold and cracked merrily. He looked up at Lisa, his eyes reflecting the nascent flames, and she felt a corresponding spark within her own chest.

"Thank you," she said softly, not just for the fire but for the sense of home he was creating in this remote place. She moved to the small kitchen area, feeling the need to contribute to this makeshift domesticity they had found themselves in.

The provisions were sparse, but Lisa was no stranger to making do with less. She rummaged through the cabinets, pulling out cans and boxes—artifacts of the cabin's last inhabitants. With a grace born from years of adapting to ever-changing circumstances, she began to assemble a meal from what was already in the cabin and the few things Oliver had brought back from the market: a can of beans, some dried herbs, and a few potatoes that he had bought. There were a couple of chicken breasts that she could add as well.

Oliver watched her from his position by the fire, the orange glow painting his rugged features in a light that seemed to soften the edges of his strong jaw. The sight of her there, humming under her breath as she worked, struck a chord with him. It was something akin to admiration, mixed with a deeper emotion that he had yet to acknowledge fully.

"Smells good," he commented, standing up to stretch his back. "You've got quite the touch, Lisa."

She glanced over her shoulder, offering him a smile that reached her warm eyes. "It's nothing fancy, but it'll keep us going."

As the fire grew stronger, its heat weaving through the space between them, so too did the bond that had been quietly strengthening since their fraught journey to this place. They moved around one another in the small cabin with an ease that belied the complexity of their situation.

"Let's eat by the fire," Lisa suggested, her voice lighter than it had been in days. There was something about the flickering flames that promised more than warmth; they offered a momentary reprieve from the world outside—a world where Trey's shadow loomed large.

"Perfect," Oliver agreed, arranging the worn cushions on the floor into a semblance of seating. Together, they settled down next to the hearth, the meal spread out before them on an old wooden board serving as an impromptu table.

In the glow of the fire, with the simple food warming them from the inside out, Oliver and Lisa found a moment of peace. It was a temporary balm, a fleeting slice of normalcy, but it was theirs—and in the vast uncertainty of their lives, it was a treasure beyond measure.

Oliver speared a chunk of the chicken with his fork, the orange light from the fire casting dancing shadows across his face. He chewed thoughtfully for a moment before a chuckle rumbled in his chest.

"You know," he began, his eyes reflecting the flames as they flickered, "when I was a kid, there was this one spot by the docks where all us local troublemakers would fish for hours, even during the school week."

Lisa watched him, her spoon halfway to her mouth, captivated. The softness of his eyes seemed at odds with the rugged lines of his face, etched from years battling the sea.

"Ever get caught?" she asked, the corner of her mouth quirking up.

"More than once." Oliver's grin widened. "Old Man Henley used to chase us off with threats of calling our folks, telling us we had to be in school. But we'd be back the next day, same as ever." His shoulders shook with laughter. "I think he secretly enjoyed the company."

"Sounds like you were quite the rebel," Lisa teased, her eyes twinkling in the dim light.

"Only when it came to fish," he admitted, and his expression softened. "That town... it's part of me, you know? The people, the sea—it's where I learned what it means to stand by someone. Guess that's why I couldn't leave you to face Trey alone."

Her heart swelled, and a warmth that had nothing to do with the fire spread through her. Setting down her bowl, Lisa drew her knees up to her chin, her arms wrapped around them.

"I grew up in many places," she began, her voice hesitant but gaining strength. "Always moving, never settling. My dad's job took us everywhere, so a place to call home...." She trailed off, lost in memories.

"Never had one?" Oliver asked softly, leaning in closer.

"Never long enough to make it feel real," she replied. "That's partly why this town, our little community here, means so much. It's the closest thing to a home I've ever had." She met his gaze, her own eyes glistening. "And meeting you, finding someone who actually cares... it's more than I ever hoped for."

"Lisa," Oliver said, his tone earnest, "you've got a home now—with me. We'll get through this together."

Their shared laughter and tears mingled with the crackling of the fire, weaving an unspoken promise between them—a promise of support, understanding, and a newfound home in each other's hearts.

The chill of the night nipped at their cheeks as Oliver led Lisa outside, his hand gently enclosing hers. They stepped onto the rough-hewn porch of the cabin, where the world opened up above them—a canvas of inky blackness peppered with a million points of light.

"Look at that," Lisa whispered, her voice filled with awe. The constellations hung overhead like celestial guardians, silent and watchful. She leaned back against the railing, her hazel eyes reflecting the stars' shimmering dance. Oliver stood beside her, his gaze not just on the heavens but lingering on her profile, illuminated by the soft glow of the cabin windows.

"Beautiful, isn't it?" he said, his breath visible in the air. "Out here, away from everything, it's like we can see all the way to the edge of the universe."

Lisa nodded, her hand tightening around his. "It feels like we're a part of something endless," she added, the vastness of the sky echoing the depth of her emotions. For a moment, they were just two souls, intertwined by fate, standing against the backdrop of eternity.

Oliver reached into his pocket and pulled out something small and metallic. It caught the glint of the stars as he held it out to her. "I want you to have this," he said, the excitement in his voice palpable.

Lisa turned to face him, curiosity lighting her features. In his palm lay a delicate silver chain, and from it dangled a pendant—an intricately crafted fish that seemed to swim in the starlight. Her fingers brushed over the cool metal, tracing the lines that brought the tiny creature to life.

"It's beautiful, Oliver," she breathed out, touched by the unexpected gift.

"It's from back home," he explained, his eyes earnest. "A local artist makes them. It's supposed to bring good luck to those who hold the sea close to their hearts."

Her smile broadened, knowing the thought he'd put into choosing something so significant. He understood her—her yearning for belonging, for something constant in the fluidity of life. This pendant, a symbol of his world, of the sea that defined him, was an offering of his love.

"Help me put it on?" Lisa asked, turning her back to him and lifting her hair off her neck.

As Oliver fastened the clasp, his fingers lightly brushed her skin, sending a ripple of warmth down her spine. She turned back around and caught his gaze, seeing the reflection of their shared journey in his eyes. Here, under the endless dome of the night, Lisa felt anchored.

"Thank you, Oliver," she said, her voice a blend of gratitude and affection. "For this, for being here with me... for everything."

He wrapped his arms around her, pulling her close. "There's nowhere else I'd rather be," Oliver murmured into her hair. And as they stood there, embracing under the watchful stars, the rest of the world—with its dangers and uncertainties—seemed to fade away. They had each other, and that was more than enough for now.

Lisa's fingers trembled slightly as she reached into her bag, drawing out a leather-bound journal, its edges worn from countless openings and closings. The dim glow of the cabin's firelight danced across the surface, highlighting the creases that told of a life well contemplated.

"Here," she said softly, passing the journal to Oliver. "This... it's my past, my hopes—everything I am and wish to be."

Oliver's hand closed gently around the offering, his touch conveying reverence for the trust she placed in him. He opened the cover, the pages emitting a faint, musty scent—a testament to their age and the journey they'd been on.

As he leafed through the pages, Lisa nestled beside him, her head finding a familiar rest against his shoulder. Together, they began to wander through her memories, her musings spilling forth in the hushed tones of shared secrets.

"Listen to this part." Oliver's voice was warm, filled with a mix of amusement and admiration as he read aloud a passage in which Lisa recounted an implausible dream she'd had—of flying over the town like a watchful guardian.

They laughed, the sound mingling with the crackle of the fire as if the flames themselves were chuckling along. It felt freeing—laughing about something so whimsical, so detached from the gravity of their current situation.

The journal's pages turned, and with them, the mood shifted. Oliver's voice caught on a sentence, a dream Lisa had penned down with such raw yearning that it seemed to echo in the cabin's corners. It was a vision of a future filled with love and safety, a place where fear didn't linger like a shadow.

"Did you ever think you'd find that place?" Oliver asked, his eyes seeking hers in the firelight.

Lisa met his gaze, her own eyes swirling with emotions. "I think I'm starting to," she whispered, her words barely louder than the rustling of the journal's pages.

Tears welled up, unbidden but not unwelcome, as they continued to explore the depths of her heart laid bare upon the paper. There were tears for the pain of days gone by and the beauty of dreams unfurling in the present moment.

"Thank you for sharing this with me," Oliver said, his voice thick with emotion. He closed the journal and set it aside, his arm wrapping around her in a silent vow of protection.

"Thank you for being someone I can share it with," Lisa replied, leaning into his embrace.

In the flickering light, surrounded by echoes of laughter and whispers of dreams, their connection deepened, roots intertwining like the intricate patterns of their lives charted across the worn pages of the journal. In that small, secluded cabin, they found solace not just in the stars above or in the warmth of the fire but in the shared experiences and aspirations they held between them.

The cabin's wooden floorboards creaked softly under their feet as Oliver reached for an old portable radio perched on the mantle. With a deft twist of the dial, a gentle and inviting melody flowed into the room. It was an old tune that carried the nostalgia of countless forgotten dances. Lisa watched him, her heart fluttering like a captured bird within her chest. The warmth from the fireplace painted his features in shades of gold and amber, highlighting the rugged lines of his face.

"May I have this dance?" Oliver asked, extending his hand with a bashful grin that belied his solid frame and the strength in his calloused fingers.

Lisa's response was a shy smile, her hand slipping into his. She stood, her movements tentative yet trusting. As they found their rhythm, the rest of the world seemed to fade—the looming threat of Trey, the uncertainty of tomorrow—all dissolving into the crackling hum of the fire and the soft crooning from the old radio.

Oliver led with a gentle surety, guiding her in a slow waltz that echoed the ebb and flow of distant ocean tides. Lisa followed, her steps growing more confident, buoyed by the sincerity in Oliver's eyes. There was something unspoken in the way he held her close, a promise that extended beyond the dance, beyond the walls of the cabin itself. Her body moved in sync with his, each turn and sway a wordless conversation that only their hearts could decipher.

And then, as the song drew to a close, Oliver pulled her closer still. His breath was warm against her cheek, his voice a low rumble that resonated within her.

"Lisa," he whispered, and it was all the invitation she needed.

Their lips met in a tender kiss, hesitant at first, like the delicate touch of a petal against skin. But as the initial shyness melted away, passion swelled between them, a surging tide that filled every crevice of doubt and fear. Lisa's arms wrapped around Oliver's neck, drawing him nearer, and he responded in kind, his embrace enveloping her in a cocoon of desire and affection.

In that kiss, their emotions intertwined, a passionate embrace that spoke of new beginnings and shared dreams. The shadows danced around them, the fire's glow a silent witness to the birth of something profound and beautiful. Oliver and Lisa, two souls adrift in a tempestuous world, found harbor in each other's arms, their first kiss sealing a bond that felt as ancient as the stars overhead—heartwarming and exciting in its purity, its promise of tomorrow.

As their lips parted, Lisa's heart beat with the timbre of a bird's wings in flight, anticipation coiling tight within her chest. She glanced at Oliver, his profile etched with determination, the set of his jaw telling her all she needed to know about his protective instincts. They were each other's sanctuary, bound by a love that had weathered tempests both literal and metaphorical. In these mountains, away from the world that didn't understand the silence between spoken words, they could be just Lisa and Oliver—no past, no threats, only the here and now.

Without another word, Oliver closed the distance between them again, his hands cradling her face with a reverence that belied the strength in his calloused fingers. Lisa's breath hitched, caught in the gravity of the moment as her own hands rose to rest against his broad chest.

Then, their lips met once again, and the world fell away.

The kiss was a confluence of everything they were—passionate yet tender, a testament to the journey they had embarked on together. It spoke of late-night whispers, shared dreams, and battles fought side by side. Their mouths moved in harmony, telling a story only they could understand, a narrative written in the language of heartbeats and stolen breaths.

Lisa melted into him, every fear and doubt evaporating in the heat of their embrace. Oliver's arms wrapped around her, strong and unyielding, a fortress built not of stone but of love and iron-clad promises. And as they stood there, lost in each other, the woods around them seemed to sigh in contentment, the trees bearing witness to a love so profound it echoed through the very roots of the earth.

Oliver's touch drifted from Lisa's cheek to the delicate curve of her jaw, tracing lines of affection with a softness that made her shiver. In the quiet of the cabin, his fingertips seemed to whisper secrets only her skin could understand—stories of longing, of nights spent yearning for this closeness. His gaze held hers, deep and fathomless, like the ocean he once called home, now anchored in the harbor of her eyes.

Her pulse quickened, a rhythmic drumbeat echoing through the cabin's stillness. Oliver's hands, those of a craftsman, moved with an artist's intent. He knew her body as one knows a cherished melody, every note and pause memorized, each touch a symphony of discovery. Lisa felt the heat bloom within her, a fragrant rose unfurling its petals under the sun's caress.

With every gentle exploration, the air between them thickened, charged with electricity that danced upon her skin. Oliver's tenderness was a balm, soothing away the scars of her past, reminding her that here, in his arms, she found sanctuary.

Lisa's breath caught in her throat as his hands traced the curve of her waist, stoking the embers of desire into a blaze. They stood together, entwined in a dance as old as time yet as fresh as the dew clinging to the morning leaves. Each touch was a promise, each glance a vow, reaffirming their love in the silent language of touch and sight.

As Oliver's fingers lingered, igniting fires with every stroke, Lisa's world narrowed to the here and now, where danger was a distant thought and love was a tangible force wrapping around them like the very air they breathed. In the embrace of the mountains, their passion blossomed, heartwarming and thrilling, suspenseful and all-consuming, a testament to the unyielding bond they shared.

Oliver's fingers hesitated at the hem of Lisa's shirt, his gaze locking with hers, a silent question hanging in the air. Her nod was subtle but sure, and the fabric whispered its ascent as it lifted over her head, breaking the barrier that separated skin from skin. The cool breath of the cabin caressed her exposed shoulders, heightening the intensity of Oliver's warm touch.

His hands were paradoxically gentle as they undressed her, each movement deliberate, dismantling not only her attire but the walls she had built around her heart. With every button undone and every zipper lowered, Lisa felt more exposed—not just to the elements of the secluded woods but to the raw emotions that Oliver evoked within her.

The carpet underfoot served as their bed, the wooden cabin their guardian. The scent of earth mingled with the faint musk of their arousal, an olfactory symphony that played to the rhythm of their racing hearts.

Oliver's shirt fell away with an ease that spoke of his familiarity with the motion, yet there was nothing routine about this moment. Each discarded garment peeled back another layer of vulnerability, revealing not just flesh but the very essence of their beings.

Lisa's hands trembled slightly as she worked at

the belt of Oliver's jeans, the clink of the buckle loud in the hushed reverence of the cabin. He stepped out of them with a grace that belied his sturdy frame, standing before her as if he were part of the land-scape—strong and unyielding, yet a part of something much larger than themselves.

The forest outside seemed to hold its breath, watching, witnessing this union of souls, a testament to their resilience and the power of love. The trees rustled softly, whispering secrets as old as time, and for a moment, the world outside their sanctuary ceased to exist.

The chill of the air contrasted with the warmth emanating from Oliver's skin as his lips grazed the tender expanse of Lisa's neck. She tilted her head back, an invitation to the affection she craved, her pulse quickening beneath the surface of her soft skin. His gentle and unhurried kisses were like raindrops in a drought—each one sending shivers cascading down her spine, awakening every nerve ending with the promise of more.

With each caress, Oliver etched a path of longing that coiled deep within Lisa, igniting a fire that had been carefully guarded. Her breaths grew heavy, laced with the thrill of their seclusion. She felt the strength in his hands, those of a man who had wres-tled with the sea, now exploring her with a reverence that spoke to the depth of his love for her.

Her fingers found their way into his hair—short and dark like the shadows that played between the trees around them. The forest was alive with the whispers of leaves, yet all she could hear was her heart thumping against the stillness. Lisa clung to him, her touch a silent plea for closeness that only he could answer.

Oliver's exploration was a journey over familiar terrain, yet each brush of his fingertips was as thrilling as the first discovery. Muscles that had tensed in readiness for danger now softened under his touch, yielding to the excitement of the moment. The suspense of what lay ahead was tantalizing, a crescendo building within her, each of his movements fanning the flames of anticipation.

In the quiet of the cabin, where shadows danced with light, their connection was palpable, a tapestry woven from threads of passion and the unspoken bond they shared. It was as if the very earth beneath them was holding its breath, bearing witness to the unfolding of their love—an intimate ballet set to the rhythm of their beating hearts.

Oliver's hands traced the curve of Lisa's spine, drawing her closer until the space between them became a memory. With each breath, their bodies seemed to move in a delicate rhythm, finding harmony in the shared silence around them. The heartbeat of the cabin pulsed beneath their feet, setting the tempo for their dance—a dance that belonged only to them, an intimate waltz whispered through every touch and gaze.

Lisa felt the world narrow down to the circle of

Oliver's arms, the steady strength that had weathered storms both literal and emotional. His body was a shield against the chill of the evening, but it was his soul that enfolded hers, warming her from within. As they moved together, the lingering fears that clung to the edges of her mind—shadows of past hurts, whispers of danger lurking beyond the tree line—melted away under the intensity of their connection.

With every movement, every connection, they climbed higher, the world shrinking until it was no larger than the space between their two hearts. Lisa's fingers dug into Oliver's shoulders, anchoring herself to him as waves of ecstasy crashed over her. The raw intensity in his eyes reflected the depth of his emotion, a mirror to the tempestuous sea churning within her own soul.

And then, as if cresting the peak of a mighty mountain, they reached the zenith of their passion. Their bodies trembled together, a shared quake that resonated through the earth beneath them. Lisa could feel the powerful beats of Oliver's heart through the heat of his chest, each thump a testament to the love that bound them irrevocably together. The energy that surged through them was fierce enough to light up the night.

In the aftermath, the world slowly returned, the sounds of the forest surrounding the cabin creeping back into awareness—the distant hoot of an owl, the rustle of leaves, the steady rhythm of the universe.

But for now, those were mere whispers compared to the symphony that had just played out between them.

They lay entwined, cocooned in the old cabin that had witnessed the timeless dance of their union. Oliver's fingers traced lazy circles on Lisa's back, a soothing gesture that spoke of a deep and abiding affection. She rested her head against his shoulder, breathing in the scent of pine from his skin, the fragrance forever interwoven with memories of this night.

As they held one another, Lisa felt a serenity she hadn't known in ages, a sense of completion. In this tranquil woodland haven, the ghosts of past and future worries were banished by the strength of their embrace. And in the gentle thrumming of their synchronized hearts, there was a promise—a silent vow that no matter what storms may come, they would face them as one. In the afterglow of their intimate moment, the bond between them was not just rekindled; it blazed brighter, fueled by the unspoken oaths of protection, love, and undying devotion.

The crackle of the dying fire served as a soft accompaniment to their shared silence. Outside, the Alaskan wilderness was a black canvas dotted with countless specks of light, each a silent guardian watching over the remote cabin. Lisa's head rested on Oliver's broad chest, and the steady rhythm of his heartbeat was a comforting lullaby that spoke of safety and warmth. In the protective circle of his arms, she let out a contented sigh, her breath dancing across his skin.

"Oliver," she murmured, her voice barely above a whisper, yet it cut through the stillness with the weight of the words she had kept guarded for so long. "I've spent so much of my life hiding... running... but with you, I feel like I've finally come home."

He tightened his hold on her, the rough callouses on his hands a testament to the life he'd led—a life of resilience against the relentless sea, now a bulwark against her own storms.

"Lisa, you are my light in the darkest night," he said, each word wrapped in the warmth of his affection. "I promise you, no matter what comes our way, I'll be here. We'll face it together. Forever and always."

Her hazel eyes, reflecting the dying embers, met his deep blue gaze. It was a confluence of two souls, an unspoken vow that wove them together with threads stronger than any tempest could sever. They were two hearts in quiet communion, promising without words to protect and support one another through every trial and tribulation.

The moment was heartwarming and exciting, a delicate bubble of tranquility in a world that had been too harsh, too cold.

But reality has a way of intruding upon even the most tender of exchanges. The sudden snap of a twig outside tore through the night, shattering the serenity into a thousand shards of unease.

Oliver's body tensed beneath her, his muscles coiling like a spring, ready to defend and shield. Lisa's pulse quickened, her mind racing through all the scenarios that could have brought about that ominous sound. A silence descended, thick and heavy with anticipation, as they both strained to hear beyond the walls of their temporary sanctuary.

"Did you hear that?" Lisa's voice was a mere breath, fear threading through it like poison.

Oliver nodded slightly with his jaw set in a determined line. "Stay here," he commanded softly, moving to disentangle himself from her embrace.

But Lisa clung to him, her fingers digging into his skin. "No, we have to stick together. Remember? Together," she insisted, her resolve bolstering her trembling voice.

They sat up, every sense heightened, the memory of Trey's relentless pursuit casting a long, ominous shadow over their newfound love. Their eyes locked, and in that glance, they understood that the path ahead would be fraught with peril. But they also knew that whatever came their way, their bond would endure, for love, once declared, is not easily undone by the darkness that lurks outside.

~

Oliver's arms wrapped around Lisa with the protective ferocity of a storm-battered sea wall, their hearts hammering a shared rhythm. Outside, the unknown rustlings of the night served as a stark reminder that danger prowled just beyond the warm glow of the cabin. But inside, encircled in Oliver's embrace, Lisa felt an ember of courage flickering to life.

"Whatever it is, I will protect you," he whispered against her hair, his breath a warm contrast to the chill that seeped through the cracks in the old wooden walls. His voice was a lighthouse beam cutting through the fog and guiding her back from the edge of panic.

She lifted her chin, meeting his steady gaze. The love she saw there kindled a fire in her belly, melting away the icy fingers of dread that Trey's shadow cast over them. "I can't hear anything," Lisa said, feeling the strength of their intertwined fingers. "You think it's gone? Whatever it was?"

"Maybe it was just an animal," he said. "Guess we're both on edge."

"We can't be too careful."

They rose as one, their movements synchronized by the silent pact they'd made. With each passing second, as they prepared for what lurked outside, the cabin seemed to shrink, the walls thinning against the vastness of their ordeal.

But their closeness grew, a tangible force that fortified their resolve.

"Remember the first time we met?" Lisa asked, her attempt at lightness clear in her voice, "You said you were no hero."

Oliver managed a wry smile, the corner of his mouth lifting in a hint of defiance against their grim reality.

"Guess I lied," he said, the twinkle in his eye belying the gravity of their situation.

"Best lie you ever told," Lisa replied, letting the momentary levity bolster her spirit.

Oliver reached over and turned on the old radio again. A flimsy thread of music drifted through the air, a melancholy melody that seemed to mourn the loss of their short-lived peace. Yet, as they swayed slightly to the tune, their bodies instinctively finding the rhythm amid chaos, it also reminded them of the joy they found in each other's arms.

"Look at us, dancing at the end of the world," Oliver murmured, his lips grazing her forehead.

"Then let's dance like we mean it," Lisa challenged softly, her eyes shining with unshed tears and determination.

And so, they stood, holding each other, moving to an unheard rhythm that pulsed like a heartbeat through the room. In the face of the approaching threat, their dance became a silent vow, a declaration that they would not be undone by fear or fate.

The distant noise that had shattered their solace now served to fuse their resolve. They were two hearts beating against the darkness, ready to confront whatever lay ahead because they knew that together, they were more than the sum of their parts. Together, they were unstoppable.

Until the past finally caught up with them.

Chapter Eleven

Oliver's heavy boots thudded against the worn wooden floorboards of the cabin as he paced back and forth. His broad, calloused hands found their way to his hips, then slid up to rake through his short, dark hair, a physical manifestation of the worry that knotted his stomach. He paused occasionally, straining to see the familiar sight of Lisa's face as she approached the cabin.

His gaze, as deep and turbulent as the ocean he knew so well, flickered constantly to the window, searching the snow-dusted path that led to the outside world. The fading light cast long shadows across the room, shadows that seemed to stretch and reach for him with spectral fingers, tightening the grip of concern around his heart. Lisa had gone outside to get wood for the fireplace. Oliver said he could do it, but she insisted. She needed the air, and she needed to go outside for once since being cooped up in the cabin for days was about to drive her nuts. That's how she had put it.

"And you don't want to see me go nuts; I promise you that much."

So, he had complied. The stack of wood was in a small shed at the end of the property. It wouldn't take her long to get back. Still, he worried. Lisa wasn't used to these mountains. She could easily get lost or maybe encounter a wild animal.

I should have gone with her. I should have insisted on going too and not let her talk me into her going alone.

The sudden crunch of tires on gravel snapped Oliver from his reverie. He lurched toward the frosted glass pane, his breath fogging a patch as he pressed close, eyes wide, hoping to catch a glimpse of that captivating smile, that wavy brown hair. Instead, his heart skidded to a halt before thundering anew as he saw a vehicle approach and Trey Montgomery stepping out, his blond hair neatly combed, the setting sun casting an eerie halo around his figure.

For a moment, time stood still. The charm that Trey wielded like a shield did nothing to mask the coldness of his eyes. Oliver knew him for what he really was. A shiver that had nothing to do with the Alaskan chill ran down Oliver's spine, and a sense of dread settled in his gut like an anchor. Oliver's protective instincts, honed by years of braving stormy waters, surged to the forefront.

As the sound of the closing car door echoed off

the trees, the twilight silence hung heavy in the air. Oliver stood motionless at the window, every muscle tensed, his mind racing with possibilities. He knew one thing for sure: he would stand between Lisa and whatever storm Trey brought with him. Oliver's love for her, as vast and unyielding as the sea, would not allow anything less.

With a deep breath, Oliver unlatched the door, the creak of the hinges slicing through the tense silence. His jaw was set, his stance firm as if bracing against an oncoming gale.

"Trey," he said, his voice edged with a storm brewing just beneath the surface, "what are you doing here?"

Trey stood there, looking like a salesman ready to peddle false hopes and broken dreams. The setting sun threw shadows across his face, lending a somber cast to his usually charismatic features.

"Oliver," he began, his voice softened in a way that didn't quite reach his eyes. "I need to talk to her."

Oliver's heart clutched within his chest, a fish caught in a net of fear and confusion. "She doesn't want to see you. She's made that very clear to me. So, you better go back now."

"No, wait," Trey said, grabbing Oliver's arm as he was about to leave. "You don't understand. It's not how she says it is. She's been lying to you, Oliver. She hasn't told you the truth."

Oliver stared at Trey, nostrils flaring. What was he talking about? "I don't believe you."

"But you have to... for her sake," Trey said. "Oliver, she... she needs help. She's sick."

Oliver paused. A frown grew between his eyes. "What do you mean by sick?"

"It's... It's cancer, Oliver." Trey's lips curved into a sorrowful frown, though his gaze remained as calculating as ever. "She got the diagnosis a few months ago. That's why she ran off. She left to save her family from the pain of it all, the slow decline. She wanted to spare us, her family, the people who love her, the hurt of watching her fade away. But we never wanted that. We want her home."

The words hung between them, heavy as the damp seaside fog. Oliver could feel the warmth of his own breath against the chill evening air, his thoughts racing like the tide against the shore. He knew Lisa— knew the weight she carried in her warm eyes, the resilience woven into her quiet strength. But this? This was a squall he hadn't seen brewing on the horizon.

Lisa was sick?

Oliver's eyes ballooned with shock, the weight of Trey's claim pressing against his chest like an anchor.

They had walked inside the cabin, and Oliver stood by the fireplace, leaning on the wall for support. His pulse throbbed in his ears, a cacophony of waves crashing against the rocky doubts that now littered his mind. Lisa, with her gentle spirit and quiet fortitude, battling cancer? It seemed as improbable as a sunken ship rising from the ocean's depths.

"Lisa wouldn't just leave her children," Oliver managed to say, his voice caught between the gale of disbelief and the undertow of concern. "Not just like that."

Trey's expression softened, the evening shadows painting him with feigned empathy.

"Oliver, you know how Lisa is. She's always thinking about everyone else. She didn't want her last memories with me and her children tainted by the specter of her illness. She didn't want them to see her fade away or to see the grief in their eyes as they clung to her until she was gone."

He stepped closer, his presence encroaching like fog rolling over the water. "She wanted to be remembered for the smiles, not the suffering."

Oliver's heart was a vessel on stormy seas, tossed between suspicion and sorrow. He could almost see Lisa there, her wavy hair dancing in the wind and those brown eyes reflecting a world of unspoken pain. The idea of her enduring such a silent battle scraped at his soul, leaving raw the notion that he hadn't been there to navigate the troubled waters with her.

"Think about it," Trey continued, his voice a

siren's call amidst Oliver's turbulent emotions. Wouldn't she want us all to remember her as she was, full of life and grace?"

Memories of Lisa's smile flickered through Oliver's mind, igniting a spark of defiance against the dark tide of Trey's manipulation. She had become a light in the small town's close-knit community, a lighthouse guiding Oliver through his own personal fogs.

"Lisa's stronger than you give her credit for," Oliver said, the warmth of his resolve shining through the cavernous doubt. "If this is true, she'll need people who care about her and will fight alongside her. She chose this path for a reason, Trey. Try to understand that. We need to respect her wishes."

Trey's eyes shifted, a glint of annoyance surfacing like a shark fin above water. But he maintained his composure, cloak-and-dagger concern still draped across his shoulders.

"Of course," Trey replied, voice smooth as glassy seas. "But you try to explain that to the children. I need to talk to her and tell her I can handle it. I'm there for her; if she still wants to stay away, then so be it. But I never got to tell her this; I never got the chance to tell her that I'm there for her, no matter what the road brings. It's important that she knows. Can't you understand that? I'm desperate here. I don't understand why she won't fight it. She needs treatment. She needs to see her doctor."

Oliver clenched his jaw, the muscles in his neck tightening like the ropes he used to anchor his fishing vessel against the capricious tides. Once a sanctuary of solitude and quiet contemplation, the cabin now felt like a trap, the walls closing in with each of Trey's revelations.

He couldn't believe it. Why hadn't Lisa told him?

Because she didn't want anyone to know, she didn't want me to pity her or see her as a patient instead of the beautiful woman she is.

"Show me," Oliver demanded, the words cutting through the air as sharply as a gutting knife. "If Lisa's sick, I want to see the proof—medical records, something—anything."

The request landed between them, heavy as an anchor sinking to the ocean floor. For a moment, the only sound was the crackle of the fireplace, its warm glow belying the cold standoff unfolding in its midst.

Trey's demeanor shifted subtly, the charm in his face retreating like the ebb of a low tide, revealing the murky seabed beneath. "Oliver, you know paperwork won't change anything. Why can't you just trust what I'm telling you?"

"Because trust isn't given freely in these waters," Oliver replied, his voice steady despite his swirling emotions. "It's earned. And you, Trey, haven't earned a damn thing. I know about your past. The women you dated, they... you abused them."

Trey's eyes flickered, their green depths darkening, clouds rolling over what had been a clear sky. His hands clasped together, not in a plea but in a calculated pose, as if he were trying to sell a faulty compass to an experienced sailor.

"Oliver, you're letting your feelings cloud your judgment," Trey said, his tone edged with a warning as sharp as winter winds cutting across the bay. "Lisa is sick. She is very, very sick."

"Respect is grounded in truth," Oliver countered, his stance unwavering like the lighthouse standing sentinel at the edge of town. "And without proof, your words are nothing more than foghorns blaring into the void."

The silence that fell upon them then was charged, a thunderstorm on the horizon waiting to break. Trey's charismatic mask had slipped enough to reveal the storm behind the facade, a tempest of frustration that Oliver had refused to navigate blindly.

"Fine," Trey spat out, the word tossed like a pebble into a still pond, its ripples distorting the reflection of the reality Oliver sought. "Think what you will, Oliver. But remember, you're not family. You're an outsider in this."

Oliver's heart thrummed in his chest, a drumbeat calling him to action. He knew the road ahead would be fraught with hidden shoals and treacherous currents, but his love for Lisa was as unyielding as the coastal pines that weathered the fiercest gales.

"Maybe so," Oliver said, his voice rising with the courage that came from knowing he fought for love and truth. "But I'll be damned if I let you navigate

Lisa's course without a true bearing. I'll find the proof myself."

With those final words hanging like a promise in the chilled air, the two men stood, locked in a silent battle of wills, their intentions as opposing as the pull between the moon and the tides. Oliver's resolve burned bright in his eyes, a flare in the encroaching dusk, ready to pierce through any deception that dared to shroud the truth.

Oliver clenched his jaw, his hands balled into fists at his sides as he took a step closer to Trey. The floorboards creaked underfoot like a ship groaning against the storm. "You won't harm her," he said, the words edged with a steely resolve that mirrored the glint of the fading sunlight against the cabin's worn windowpanes.

Trey's eyes narrowed, the green in them darkening like the forest canopy at dusk. "You're out of your depth here, fisherman. I'm not here to harm her. I'm here to tell her I love her and to come home."

"Am I?" Oliver's voice carried the weight of the ocean's waves, relentless and unforgiving. "Because I see right through you, Trey. You prey on the vulnerable, but Lisa isn't alone. Not anymore."

The air between them crackled, charged with the electricity of an impending storm. Trey took a half-step back, his composure beginning to fracture like thin ice beneath a heavy boot.

"Lisa needs someone who'll fight for her and put her first," Oliver continued, his voice rising with the crescendo of his emotions. Each syllable was a whitecap breaking against the shore, powerful and unyielding. "And I swear to you, I will uncover the truth. I will keep her safe."

Trey's lips twitched into a semblance of a smirk, but it faltered, unable to hold its shape against the tide of Oliver's conviction. Oliver saw the flicker of uncertainty cross Trey's face, a momentary lapse that revealed the chink in his armor.

"Good luck with that," Trey scoffed, though the bravado rang hollow. "And just how are you going to keep her safe from a disease that is slowly killing her from the inside?"

"I need you to leave," Oliver said. "If Lisa wants to see you, she will come find you."

Trey snorted angrily, but Oliver stood tall in front of him, towering over him. Trey backed away, then went and sat in a chair. "I'm staying here until I have seen Lisa. I'm not leaving until she tells me to."

Oliver watched him, his chest heaving with exertion as if he'd been battling the very forces of nature. A gust of wind swept through the open door, carrying the promise of rain and the scent of distant shores. Oliver closed his eyes momentarily, letting the cool breeze wash over him.

He opened them again, the determination in his heart as clear and fierce as the blue that stretched endless and deep in his gaze. For Lisa, he would weather any storm.

Trey's stance stiffened, the lines of his face hardening as he recognized the futility of sweet talk and half-truths. "You don't get it, do you?" His voice was a low growl, the charm stripped away to reveal a threat lurking beneath. "Stay away from Lisa, Oliver. This is your final warning. You have no idea what you're meddling with."

The air in the cabin seemed to drop a few degrees, and the light dimmed as clouds gathered outside, casting shadows across the wooden floorboards. Oliver felt the weight of Trey's warning like an anchor pulling at his resolve, but he wouldn't let fear sink him.

"Threats won't work on me, Trey," Oliver replied, his voice steady as bedrock. He met Trey's gaze, his own eyes reflecting the tumultuous waves of a stormy ocean. "I care about her more than you'll ever understand. And I will not stand aside while you cast your shadow over her life."

"Is that so?" Trey's lips pulled back into a sneer, revealing the predator within. "She lied to you, Oliver. She didn't tell you she was sick. She didn't tell you why she left. She deceived you... pulled you into her life and made you love her without telling you she might have to leave you soon."

"Mark my words," Oliver continued, unflinching, the timbre of his voice carrying the depth of his commitment. "I will do anything—anything—to keep her safe."

"You're so ridiculous," Trey said. "Are all men out here this stubborn and old-fashioned? You think you're all man with your weathered face and big muscles. But she's got you fooled, Oliver. And you must be angry about that."

Silence hung between them, filled only by the sound of their breath and the distant rumble of thunder.

The standoff ended not with words but with the tacit acknowledgment of a battle line drawn. Trey's expression clouded, the threat in his eyes as clear as the coming storm. But Oliver stood resolute, the lighthouse standing guard over treacherous waters, unwavering and ever watchful.

The standoff hung heavy as a fog; the two men locked in an unspoken duel. Oliver's jaw set firm, his stance rooted like an ancient pine against the howl of a merciless wind, while Trey's posture was that of a hawk perched, ready to swoop with lethal precision. Without a word, their eyes held each other's—Oliver's deep blue, steady and unwavering; Trey's green, flickering with the dark flame of intent.

In those prolonged seconds, the world seemed to shrink to the space between them, every breath, every heartbeat amplified in the stillness. The air itself became a live wire, charged with the imminent threat of lightning yet to strike.

"I need you to leave," Oliver said. "Now."

With the suddenness of a snapped branch, Trey's glare turned icy, his lips tightening into a scornful curve. He gave a slow, deliberate blink as if to close the chapter on this confrontation, on any doubt of his resolve.

"Remember this," Trey whispered, his voice venomous silk that threatened to suffocate hope, "you're out of your depth."

Without another word, he got up, and spun on his heel, the motion carrying all the finality of a gavel's fall. He rushed out the door without shutting it behind him. His footsteps crunched on the gravel path as he strode toward the waiting car, the sound punctuating the silence like distant thunderclaps. The taillights flared red as he opened the door and slipped inside, a specter retreating from the light.

Oliver remained in the doorway, his heart pounding a relentless drumbeat of mixed emotion. Anger and fear wrestled within him alongside the fierce protectiveness that had surged to the surface like a tidal wave. He watched as the car backed away, its engine growling a low challenge before fading into the distance.

Trey's departure left a void filled only by the cacophony of questions echoing through Oliver's mind. What truths lay buried beneath Trey's revelations? Was she truly ill? If so, then it broke his heart into pieces. And anger rose in him as well. Why wouldn't she have told him? How could he shield Lisa from a threat woven so intricately into the fabric of her life?

Despite the turmoil, a glint of something indefinable sparked within him—a fusion of adrenaline and ardor, igniting a flame that would not be quenched.

He needed answers. He needed answers from Lisa.

Oliver's lungs filled with crisp evening air, the sharp intake steadying his racing heart. His fists, once clenched in suppressed fury, now unfurled as he drew on an inner well of calm as deep and mysterious as the ocean. With each breath, the chaos wrought by Trey's visit settled like silt to the ocean floor, revealing a path forward as clear as the waters on a tranquil day.

He stepped back into the cabin, his resolve hardening like the ancient pines that stood sentinel around this secluded refuge. The room, once a sanctuary shared with Lisa, now echoed with the gravity of his new purpose. Oliver's gaze swept the familiar space—the faded photograph of the town's harbor on the wall, the cushioned chair where Lisa would curl up with a smile, her soft laughter still lingering in the fibers.

"Lisa, I'll find the truth," he whispered, not to the empty room but to the promise held within those grooved chambers. "I'll peel away his deceit, layer by layer until there's nothing left to hide behind."

Chapter Twelve

Lisa's hand hesitated on the doorknob, her breath fogging in the sharp Alaskan air before she pushed open the door with one hand, carrying logs with the other. The cabin's warmth caressed her cheeks as she stepped inside and put the wood down, but the sight that greeted her sent a chill far colder than the night straight to her bones. Oliver sat slumped at the kitchen table; his normally stoic face was marred by the rivulets of tears that had carved clean paths through the day's stubble.

"Oliver?" Her voice was barely a whisper, yet it seemed to boom in the quiet of the room. She closed the distance between them with swift, determined steps, her hands reaching out instinctively as if they alone could wipe away not just his tears but the cause of them.

"Hey, what happened?" Lisa's voice trembled like

the last leaf clinging to a branch in autumn, betraying the swirl of emotions she fought to keep contained. Her gaze scanned his face—a face she knew as well as the back of her own hand, now etched with an anguish that tugged at her heartstrings.

"Talk to me," she coaxed gently, her fingertips brushing against his arm in a silent plea for him to share his burden. Oliver's eyes, so often reminiscent of calm seas, were stormy now, and it frightened her more than she cared to admit. Here, in the quiet refuge of the cabin, with the man who'd become her anchor in ways she'd never expected, vulnerability weaved its way through the timber walls, and she felt it settle around them both, an unspoken pact of trust and mutual protection in a world that seemed intent on testing their resilience.

Oliver's chest heaved, a visible battle to draw breath against the weight of his emotions. His voice, when it finally broke through, carried the tremors of barely suppressed sobs.

"Lisa," he started, the name coming out as a plea, "I didn't know what to do."

"Tell me," she urged, her own heart skipping beats as she braced herself for his words.

He clenched and unclenched his fists, the knuckles white with tension. "It was Trey," he managed to say, and the simple utterance of the name acted like a cold splash of water on Lisa's face, chilling her from within.

"What about him?" Her confusion carved deeper

lines into her forehead, her mind racing to catch up with this new, unwelcome twist.

Oliver looked at her, his eyes reflecting a storm that seemed foreign in their depths. "He came here."

"He was here?" she shrieked.

"His eyes, Lisa... they were different. And he told me something...." He swallowed hard, the effort to speak seeming to cost him more with each word.

Lisa felt a chill run down her spine. Trey's unpredictable temper was one thing, but this change in demeanor spelled a new kind of danger. Oliver's admission sent her thoughts spiraling, the small cabin suddenly feeling far less like a haven and more like a trap with walls too close for comfort. She fought to keep her expression steady, to be the rock that Oliver now needed, just as he had been for her countless times before.

"Oliver, look at me," she said, her voice softer now but threaded with an undercurrent of urgency.

As his gaze met hers, she sought to convey every ounce of courage she felt blooming within her chest. It was a silent vow that no matter what darkness Trey brought to their doorstep, they would face it together.

"What happened?"

And just as she said the words, the sound of a car door shutting outside caused her heart to race in her chest.

"Oliver, is that him? Is he back?"

~

Lisa's fingers twitched at her sides, the air in the cabin thick with a tension that settled like an unseen fog. She took a step back, her heart pounding a staccato rhythm against her ribs. The rustic charm of the quaint hideaway they had once found solace in now seemed to mock her with its sturdy oak beams and the cheerful crackle from the fireplace.

Her eyes, usually so warm and inviting, became sharp sentinels, flitting from window to shadowed corner and back again. Each creak of the wooden floorboards, each whisper of movement from the dancing flames, sent jolts of fear through her already taut nerves. The space between the old grandfather clock and the mahogany bookshelf suddenly appeared as a potential route, a narrow path to safety. But it was too far, too exposed.

He was coming for her. She knew he was.

There was the back door, partially obscured by the heavy drapes that Oliver loved for their ability to block out the rest of the world. Now, those same drapes seemed to close in on her, suffocating, as if conspiring with the fates to keep her trapped.

She looked at Oliver, the confusion growing on her face.

"We need to go, Oliver."

"Why?" Oliver asked.

"What do you mean why?" she asked desperately.

"You never explained to me why you're running from him," Oliver said.

"I don't have time to explain it all now," she said. "Come on. Let's get out the back."

"You lied to me."

"Not now, Oliver. We need to go."

"Why? Because you don't want him to remind you that you have children and a responsibility? Because you're sick?"

"What are you talking about?" Lisa said. "We need to go. Now!"

"Looking for a way out, Lisa?" Trey's voice sliced through the silence like a blade. Devoid of the warmth she had once known in those eyes, now flat and unyielding as polished stone, his calm was unsettling, a stark contrast to the tremor that claimed her limbs.

She turned slowly, her breath catching in her throat at the sight of him. Trey stood there, the epitome of control, his blond hair immaculately swept back, his face a mask of serenity that belied the darkness lurking beneath.

"T-Trey?"

"Hello there, wifey," he said. "It's been a minute, hasn't it?"

"Trey, you have no right to...." She looked at Oliver, who wasn't doing anything. He just sat there with his eyes welled up in tears.

What's wrong with him?

Lisa backed up, and Trey grabbed her wrist forcefully. "Oliver? Help... please?"

Oliver looked up at them, a puzzled look in his eyes. "What are you doing, Trey?"

"Taking back what's mine."

Oliver rose to his feet, a frown growing between his eyes. Then he looked at Trey, and his heart stopped.

In Trey's hand, which hung casually by his side, was a gun. Its black metal surface glinted ominously in the firelight, a sinister promise in his otherwise passive stance.

The sight of the weapon, so incongruous in the homey setting, pulled a gasp from his lips. Lisa's mind screamed for action, but her body felt rooted to the spot. The gentle demeanor that had always been her shield was now a liability in the face of cold steel and colder intentions.

Trey's smile didn't reach his eyes as he took a measured step forward. "Don't look so surprised," he drawled, the gun lifting slightly as though in punctuation to his words. "You must've known this was coming."

Lisa's pulse thrummed in her ears, the sound drowning out the crackle of the fire, the ticking of the clock, everything but the blood roaring its frantic plea for survival. Oliver's presence behind her, steady and solid, was the only comfort she dared allow herself as she faced down the barrel of Trey's intentions.

"Whatever you're thinking, Trey," she said, her voice steadier than she felt, "it doesn't have to end this way."

The room held its breath, waiting for his reply.

Lisa's breath hitched, the air in the cabin thickening with dread. She could feel the weight of Oliver's gaze on her, silent questions and concerns hanging unspoken between them. Her mind, once a sanctuary of quiet contemplation, was now a torrent of fear and strategy, casting about for any edge they might use to survive.

"Oliver," she whispered, barely audible over the hammering of her heart. The name was both a plea and a talisman, invoking the strength she had seen in him, time and again, the resilience of a man who'd weathered storms both literal and figurative.

His response was instantaneous, an embodiment of the protective instincts that were as much a part of him as the salt in his veins. With a decisive movement, he sidestepped, placing his sturdy fisherman's frame between Lisa and the chilling calm of Trey's gunpoint standoff. Deep blue eyes met hers for a fraction of a second, and in that glance, she read a world of unspoken vows, a silent promise that he would lay down his life before he let harm come to her.

"Easy, Trey," Oliver said in a low and even voice, but beneath the surface, Lisa could hear the taut undercurrent of controlled fear. "Let's talk this through."

Trey's lip curled, but his grip on the gun didn't

waver, his stance a portrait of deadly intent framed by the rustic charm of the cabin walls.

"Talk?" Trey's query sliced through the tension. "Oh, we're well past talking, don't you think?"

"There is no cancer, is there?" he asked. "It was just a way for you to manipulate me. Again."

Oliver's jaw clenched, a subtle tell that belied his outward calm. Lisa knew that look and had seen it when gale-force winds threatened to tear nets and livelihoods alike. It was the look of a man who would not—could not—back down when those he cared for were in peril.

Lisa's fingers brushed against the rough-hewn table behind her, her senses heightened to each minute texture. Her mind, ever her greatest weapon, began to map the terrain of their precarious situation: the distance to the door, the heft of objects within reach, and the split-second timing that might mean the difference between escape and catastrophe.

"Oliver...," she murmured, a wordless conveyance of trust and urgency. She knew they wouldn't get out of this by force alone; it would take cunning, speed, and an unwavering faith in each other. Oliver's slight nod was all the confirmation she needed. They were in this together, and together, they would find a way out.

Their hearts might be pounding in sync, a frantic duet of adrenaline and fear, but beneath it all ran a current of something stronger, something that the cold metal in Trey's hand could never touch. It was the warmth of shared courage, the bond of two souls united against the darkness, ready to fight for their lives and for the flicker of something that might, one day, be called love.

The cabin air, once thick with tension, now erupted into chaos as Oliver's muscles coiled, and he sprang forward like a bear protecting its cub. His form blurred into motion, a streak of protective fury aimed directly at Trey. Their bodies collided with the sound of an avalanche, raw power against sinister intent, fighting for dominion over the small, deathly piece of metal that gleamed ominously in Trey's grasp.

Lisa's breath hitched, her heart clamoring against her ribs as if to echo the violence before her eyes. She felt the rush of blood in her ears, a tidal wave of fear and adrenaline that threatened to sweep her away in its current. Yet, she stood riveted, her gaze locked on the two men entangled in their deadly dance.

Oliver's eyes flashed with a ferocity that could rival the storms he braved at sea, his every movement instinctive and desperate. There was a grace to his strength, a terrifying beauty in the way he fought— not for survival alone but for her, for them, for every promise unspoken that lingered in the charged air between them.

Trey grunted, a serpent in man's clothing, and as he sought to regain the upper hand, his face contorted in rage. The gun glinted between them, a pendulum swinging with each jostle and jab, its trajectory uncertain, its potential endgame horrifyingly clear.

"Oliver!" Lisa's voice broke through her paralysis. She prayed silently that he would emerge victorious from this grim waltz. The stakes were higher than they had ever been; there was no room for error, no second chances in this game of life and death.

She could see the strain in Oliver's jaw, the determination that set his shoulders like steel beams. He wasn't just fighting Trey; he was fighting for a future, for a chance at the normalcy and peace that had eluded them both for too long. In his struggle, there was hope, an unyielding resolve that spoke of love in its purest form—fierce, protective, unwavering.

As the two men grappled with fate, Lisa found within herself a wellspring of courage she never knew she possessed. A warm glow rose within her against the cold dread that sought to claim her spirit. She realized that this struggle, this moment, was a crucible, one that would forge the path ahead, for better or worse.

Her eyes met Oliver's in a fleeting glance, a spark of connection amidst the fray. It was a silent vow, an acknowledgment that whatever happened, their bond would not be broken by the likes of Trey. They were more than the sum of their fears; they were a force to be reckoned with, and they would not go gently into the dark night that threatened to engulf them.

The tussle was brutal and raw—a dance of survival where each step could be their last. Oliver's fingers found purchase on Trey's wrist, and Oliver twisted it with a heave that seemed to draw from the very depths of his soul.

There was a moment suspended in time like the final calm before a storm's onslaught when Trey's grip faltered. Then, as if compelled by the collective will of all who had ever faced darkness and stood firm, the gun slipped from Trey's hand and skittered across the wooden floorboards, its black sheen a stark contrast to the worn timber. It landed by the fireplace.

Lisa's breath hitched, a silent gasp lost in the thundering of her heartbeat. Her eyes, so often reflecting a world of thought and emotion, now glinted with the sharp edge of resolve. This was it—their fleeting chance. She scanned the cabin, a place once filled with the warmth of whispered secrets and shared dreams, now tainted by treachery. The door beckoned, an escape from the nightmare that had ensnared them, but it was not merely a physical barrier between danger and freedom; it was the threshold to a future they still dared to hope for.

Oliver's chest heaved, his breathing as ragged as the waves that crashed upon the town's rocky shore, yet within him burned an unwavering light—a light that guided Lisa through the fog of fear. She knew then that whatever plan sprang forth from her frantic mind would hinge upon trust, the kind built through quiet moments and tested in turmoil.

Her gaze flickered to the fallen weapon, its presence a reminder of what lay at stake. She considered their options, each scenario unfolding with the precision of a chess game where lives were the pieces and every move counted. They needed to act swiftly, decisively, before Trey could recover and the balance shifted once more. Should she go for the gun or the door? If she went for the gun, Trey might beat her to it. He was closer and had already risen to his feet, leaping for it.

But even as her thoughts raced, there was warmth in the cold clutches of terror, for beside her stood a man whose love was a shield, whose strength was her refuge. And in the chaos, Lisa Montgomery felt something akin to awe for the fisherman who had become her anchor in life's most violent storms. With Oliver, she knew they could navigate through this perilous passage, their bond an unbreakable chain that tethered them to hope, to each other, and to the promise of dawn after the longest night.

Determined blue clashed with anxious hazel in a fleeting exchange that spoke volumes. In the span of a heartbeat, Oliver's gaze conveyed a message of urgency and trust to Lisa, his eyes a mirror to their shared resolve. It was the kind of glance old friends might share before leaping into unknown waters, the kind that said, "Follow my lead," without uttering a single syllable.

With no time for words, Lisa nodded, her eyes reflecting the unspoken pact. Her heart did a quick step against her ribs, thrumming with a mixture of terror and fierce determination. She could feel the heat of the moment pressing in around them, yet within that intensity, there was a peculiar warmth that only Oliver could inspire.

She drew a breath, readying herself for what must come next. This was not the gentle rhythm of her introverted world nor the quiet solitude she often cloaked herself in; this was the raw edge of survival where every second shaped the future as distinctly as a sculptor chiseling marble.

Channeling the resilience that had carried her through so many of life's trials, Lisa tensed her muscles like a sprinter on the starting block. There would be no hesitation, no looking back. The door to the cabin, once a barrier between them and the wild, now stood as the gateway to their freedom.

With a surge of adrenaline that sent her pulse racing, Lisa sprang into action. She bolted toward the door, the floorboards creaking under the sudden weight of her resolve. Each step was a prayer, each breath a plea that Oliver would be right behind her.

As she reached the door, her hand grasping the cool metal of the knob, she dared to cast a fleeting glance over her shoulder. Her heart leaped into her throat at the sight of Oliver's sturdy form pushing off the ground, his movements fueled by protective instincts and the same powerful drive that had just propelled her forward.

The night air rushed to greet her as she flung the door open, the darkness outside both a shroud and a shield.

The night embraced Lisa and Oliver as they burst from the cabin, the stars overhead obscured by the looming threat they left behind. Their feet pounded against the earth, a staccato rhythm underscoring their shared resolve. The woods around them were alive with nocturnal whispers, but all they could hear was the thundering of their own heartbeats, synchronized in frantic tempo.

Lisa's breath came in sharp gasps, the cool air stinging her lungs with each inhalation. She felt Oliver's hand briefly touch the small of her back, an unspoken reassurance that he was there, that they were in this together. The gesture ignited a warmth within her that contrasted starkly against the icy fear threatening to claw its way into her chest.

They darted between trees, their shadows fleeting under the moon's watchful eye. Every snapped twig or rustle of leaves sent a jolt of alarm through Lisa, but she pushed forward, her legs fueled by a fierce desire to survive, to shield the man who had become her unexpected ally in this chaos.

Oliver's presence was a constant force by her side, his strength an anchor in the fluid uncertainty of their flight. They moved with a unity born of desperation, a dance of survival orchestrated by a silent promise to protect each other at any cost.

As they navigated the treacherous terrain, Lisa's thoughts raced ahead, forging pathways of escape, mapping out a future where tonight's terror was just a fading scar. She glanced at Oliver, his profile set in determination, and felt a surge of something more potent than fear... hope.

They were two souls thrown together by circumstance, bound by a thread of burgeoning trust and unspoken affection. As they fled into the enveloping darkness, with only the beat of their hearts and the strength of their will to guide them, Lisa and Oliver knew they would face it together no matter what lay ahead.

Chapter Thirteen

The dusk-laden silence of the clearing was pierced by the ominous crackle of twigs underfoot outside, a stark reminder that the refuge they had found in the heart of the woods was anything but safe. They had been on the run for a long time. They needed rest. Shadows danced against the trees surrounding them as the embers in the fire fought for life, casting an eerie glow over Lisa's delicate features. Her wavy brown hair fell like a curtain around her face, and within the safety of the dim light, her eyes shimmered with unshed tears.

Beside her, Oliver's presence was a fortress in the storm; his rugged frame seemed carved from the very wilderness that concealed them. His eyes, which so often mirrored the tranquility of the ocean he loved, now flickered with the flame of fear and vigilance. They sat huddled together, the fisherman's calloused hand covering hers, a silent promise of protection in the chill of the Alaskan night.

Each snap of a branch tightened the vise around Lisa's chest, compressing the breath from her lungs until she felt she might suffocate under the weight of her own dread. She could not live like this—perpetually haunted, forever looking over her shoulder. It was time to unload the burdens that shackled her spirit.

With a resolve born from months on the run and years of silent suffering, Lisa inhaled deeply, the cool air bracing against her lungs like a splash of icy water. She turned toward Oliver, her gaze locking onto his with an intensity that belied her gentle nature. In the quiet space between them, her lips parted, ready to voice the secrets that had long poisoned her peace.

"Oliver," she began, her voice barely above a whisper yet laden with the gravity of what was to come. "There are things about my past I've never shared with you... things I need you to know."

His expression softened, the creases of worry smoothing into lines of attentive care. He nodded, the simple gesture an anchor in the turmoil threatening to capsize her. As she drew another breath, preparing to unveil the truths that could change everything, Lisa saw something shift in Oliver's demeanor—a steeling of his soul, a readiness to weather the storm beside her.

Tears welled, blurring the edges of the man

before her, but Lisa blinked them back. She would not falter now, not when her freedom—and perhaps their lives—depended on the courage to speak. Oliver's hand squeezed hers, tethering her to the moment, to the hope that revealing her darkest hours might finally lead them toward the dawn of a new day.

"Oliver, it's about Trey...," she said, her voice gaining strength. The sorrow in her eyes mingled with fierce determination, a testament to the resilience that had carried her this far. She was ready to let him in, to trust him with the rawest parts of her story.

Lisa's hands were ice, her fingertips numb as they gripped the sleeve of his sweater covering the arms that were wrapped around her shoulders.

"It started small," she whispered, her voice barely above the crackling of the dying fire. "Trey... he was charming at first, attentive. But soon, it turned into something twisted, a possessiveness that felt like chains."

The words tumbled from her, heavy and dark, like stones into the still waters of Oliver's soul.

"He monitored my every move, Oliver. He'd make me pay for it if I spoke to someone for too long or didn't answer the phone right away. With his words, his fists...."

Oliver's jaw tensed, his eyes stormy seas reflecting the flickering firelight. He leaned closer, prompting her to continue with a nod, his presence a solid force in the darkness of the night.

"Sometimes, I woke up not knowing if I'd see the end of the day," she continued, her voice breaking on the undulating waves of her past fear. "Every creak of the floorboards and every unexpected shadow made my heart race. I lived in constant terror, and the worst part was the smiling mask I had to wear outside, pretending everything was fine."

She looked into his eyes, seeking an anchor in the tumble of her memories. Finding it in the unwavering gaze that met hers, Lisa drew strength from Oliver's silent encouragement. There was no judgment there, only a fierce protectiveness that enveloped her like a warm embrace.

"Leaving him took every ounce of courage I had," she said, a shuddering breath lifting her chest. "I waited for the right moment, getting myself ready, finding a spot on the map that was so far away I thought he wouldn't be able to find me, and one day while he was at work, I took the chance, not knowing if he was one step behind. I left everything—my family, my kids. Oh, how I miss my children, Oliver. I always believed I could come back for them. I just didn't know how. I always knew he would try and kill me if I left. I just knew it."

Oliver's strong hands clenched into fists, knuckles whitening as if restraining the urge to battle her demons himself. His empathy wove through the air between them, a tangible thing bolstering her spirit. He understood; she could see it in the way his anger was tempered with care, and his body leaned toward her, ready to stand between her and the world.

"Lisa, you're safe with me," he murmured, his voice a low rumble in the quiet night. "I'm here and won't let anyone hurt you again."

His words were a balm, soothing the raw edges of her wounds and promising safety in a life where such assurances were as rare as sunlight in an Alaskan winter. Oliver's resolve was clear, the set of his shoulders telling her he'd face down any storm for her. It was heartwarming, yet beneath it all, a thrilling undercurrent promised action should the need arise.

And in that small clearing, with darkness surrounding them, Lisa felt the first flutter of hope. Oliver's presence was a lighthouse in her darkened world, guiding her toward a harbor she'd once believed unattainable.

Lisa told him everything, all the nights she had suffered through, all the fear and terrors he had put her through while they were married, and she had tried to stick it out for the children. Her final words hung in the air, a delicate confession of her once-shattered reality. The silence in the clearing was profound—a shared sanctuary where Lisa had laid bare her soul to Oliver, and he had received it with solemn grace. They were two souls entwined by circumstance, bound by an intimate understanding of each other's pain and resilience.

But in that moment of vulnerability, a sharp crack shattered the tranquility like a stone through glass. Their heads snapped toward the source of the sound, a primal fear constricting their hearts as the noise encroached upon their secluded haven. The rustling grew louder and more insistent as if the woods themselves were conspiring to unleash chaos upon their newfound peace.

Oliver's hand found Lisa's in the dim light, his fingers interlocking with hers—a silent vow that he was there, that they were together in whatever was coming next. His pulse thrummed against her skin, a testament to the adrenaline beginning to flood his veins. Yet within the storm of trepidation, Lisa felt a sliver of warmth from the simple touch, a reminder that she was no longer alone.

Framed by the tall trees, they spotted him. Trey. His figure was menacing and terrible in its familiarity. The gun, dark and ominous, was clutched in his grip, a metallic extension of his rage. His eyes, which once could have charmed the wary, now glinted with a malevolent light that turned Lisa's blood to ice.

"Lisa," he spat her name like venom, his voice a serrated knife cutting through the quiet.

For a fraction of a second, time slowed, and Lisa observed him—the carefully groomed hair now disheveled, the lines of his face twisted in anger—this man who had once promised love but delivered only torment. Her chest tightened with dread, yet beneath it stirred a fierce determination that had carried her this far. She would not be broken again, not when she'd tasted the freedom Oliver had helped her find.

Beside her, Oliver shifted subtly, his body tensing like a coiled spring, every muscle prepared to act. His presence was a reassurance, a promise of protection that bolstered her courage. He was the shield to her vulnerability, ready to stand against the storm that was Trey.

"Leave us alone," Lisa heard herself say, her voice steady despite the tumultuous pounding of her heart. It was a demand for reclaiming her life, a life that no longer had room for the terror Trey embodied.

Trey's lip curled into a sneer, his finger twitching on the trigger as if savoring the power he wielded. But Lisa, with Oliver by her side, stood her ground, an unspoken pact between them that they would face this storm together, come what may.

In the flickering shadows of the clearing, Oliver's eyes narrowed, the secrets of the sea they held now stormy with resolve. Without hesitation, his rugged form sprang into motion, a protective barrier driven by a primal need to shield Lisa. The warmth that once radiated from him turned into fierce determination;

he was an unyielding fortress between her and the menace that loomed in front of them.

"Lisa, get back!" he barked, his voice the rumble of thunder presaging a tempest's wrath. His large fisherman's hands, calloused from years of battling the elements, reached out not for nets or ropes but for the threat that dared to breach their sanctuary.

Trey's sneer faltered. The gun, a lethal extension of his malice, trembled as Oliver's onslaught bore down on him. But hate fueled Trey's resolve, and his finger convulsed around the cold trigger.

The gunshot—a harrowing crack—shattered the strained stillness of the woods. Birds, nestled in the nearby trees, took flight in a panic, their wings beating against the canvas of the night sky.

Oliver grunted, his momentum faltering as the bullet tore through the air, an unseen predator that found its mark. He staggered, his face contorting in pain, the rugged lines that spoke of life at sea now etched with shock and agony. His knees buckled beneath him, and he crumpled to the ground, the solidity of his frame yielding to the violent kiss of lead.

"Oliver!" Lisa's cry was a sharp blade of fear, piercing the charged atmosphere. Her gentle demeanor, so often defined by quiet strength, was now alight with a desperate fervor. The captivating smile that had endeared her to the small Alaskan town was nowhere to be found, replaced by a grimace of terror and heartache. She dropped to his side, her eyes pooling with tears that mirrored the chaos unraveling around them.

Yet, even in this dire moment, the bond between Lisa and Oliver remained unbroken, their connection a light amidst the encroaching darkness. Oliver's protectiveness, though momentarily subdued by the assailant's bullet, had ignited a spark within her, a fiery will to survive stoked by his unwavering loyalty.

Lisa's fingers found Oliver's pulse, weak but present, beneath the coarse fabric of his shirt. Hope flickered in her chest, but there was no time to savor it. Trey's shadow loomed over them, his breath ragged with fury and something that might have been glee.

"Always the hero, huh?" Trey sneered, his voice a jagged edge in the stillness of the woods. "But not quick enough this time."

Her heart fractured further with each mocking word, but Lisa Montgomery was no longer just a woman haunted by ghosts of fear. The sight of Oliver, wounded and vulnerable on the ground, transformed her hesitation into resolve. She couldn't let his sacrifice be for nothing.

With the stealth borne of necessity, her gaze shifted around the area, landing on a solid rock next to her.

Adrenaline surged through her veins—an unexpected ally—and she seized the rock, its weight grounding her trembling hands. Trey's eyes were still fixed on Oliver, unaware of the storm about to break upon him.

"Look at you," Trey continued, the gun still in his grasp, a dark promise. "Pathetic."

As if drawn by a force greater than herself, Lisa rose, holding the rock high in both hands. With a swift, arching motion, she brought it crashing down toward Trey. The element of surprise was hers; the rock connected with his arm, and the sound of impact was a satisfying thud against the silence.

Trey's howl of pain filled the air and bounced against the trees, his grip on the weapon faltering as he stumbled back. For a heartbeat, Lisa locked eyes with him, her own blazing with a ferocity that belied her gentle nature. This moment, this escape, it was her doing, her victory—a testament to the strength she'd forged in fires long thought extinguished.

Without looking back, Lisa vaulted toward the tall trees, propelled by the desperate need to survive and the fierce determination to bring both her and Oliver out of this nightmare alive.

Lisa's legs pumped furiously beneath her, and the forest floor was a blur of browns and greens as she darted between trees. Her breath came in ragged gasps, clouding the cold air with each exhalation. The thudding of her heart seemed to drown out all other sounds—until the crack of branches and rustling leaves signaled that Trey was not far behind.

"Running will get you nowhere, Lisa!" His malice-laced voice cut through the quiet of the woods like a knife. "You can't escape me!"

The threat sent a shiver down her spine, but fear was no longer her master. This flight was fueled by something more potent: a blend of love for the man lying injured behind her and an unyielding desire for freedom.

With each stride, memories flooded back—the gentle touch of Oliver's hand, the warmth of his smile. It was those moments that steeled her resolve, lending strength to her limbs despite the burning in her chest.

"Come out, come out, wherever you are," Trey taunted, his footsteps a relentless rhythm in pursuit. He was playing with her the way a cat toys with a wounded bird before delivering the final blow.

But Lisa was no helpless creature. She was a woman forged by trials, shaped by the very horrors that Trey had inflicted upon her. Each labored breath was a testament to her survival, each step forward an act of defiance.

She would not falter, not now, when so much was at stake. With a surge of determination, she pushed onward, the dense canopy above casting fleeting shadows on her path. Every fiber of her being focused on one goal: to put as much distance as possible between herself and the monster that hunted her.

And in that unwavering purpose, there was a glimmer of something more than just the thrill of the chase or the terror it evoked. There was hope—a flickering light in the darkness, guiding her toward an uncertain yet promising future.

The forest whispered around her, leaves rustling encouragement with every desperate footfall. Lisa Montgomery was running, yes, but she was also racing toward a new chapter—one where fear would no longer hold sway over her heart.

Lisa's chest heaved as she darted through the underbrush, her hair snagging on the reaching fingers of wild brambles. In the orchestra of nighttime woods —a symphony of crickets and distant owls—Trey's footsteps played the ominous bass line that threatened to overwhelm her.

There was no time for fear or fatigue; she had to think quickly and be the cunning fox rather than the cornered rabbit. Her eyes, usually so gentle and inviting, now scanned the woods with the sharpness of a hawk. And there it was—a fallen tree, its once towering form now a barricade between predator and prey.

With a swift pivot, Lisa slid behind the thick trunk, her breaths shallow and quiet as a secret. She pressed her back against the rough bark, willing herself to become part of the forest's tapestry, invisible and unnoticed. The seconds stretched as she listened to the crunch of leaves and the snapping of twigs.

"Lisa, sweetheart, you can't hide from me," Trey called out, his voice laced with a mock sweetness that chilled her to the bone.

His steps drew near, each footfall a drumbeat to her racing heart. Then, silence. The hunter was close, too close. Lisa tightened her muscles like coiled springs, ready to unleash the force pent up within her slight frame.

As Trey's shadow loomed over the tree, she pushed off with all the strength her legs could muster. Bursting from her cover, Lisa struck out with a fierce determination etched into every line of her face. Her foot connected squarely with Trey's chest, the impact sending shockwaves up her leg.

"Ugh!" he gasped, stumbling back, caught off guard by her sudden defiance. The look in his eyes, usually so piercing and confident, now flickered with uncertainty. It was a momentary lapse, but it was a victory for Lisa—one forged from countless nights dreaming of freedom, of being more than just a victim.

For a heartbeat, the forest held its breath, and in that pause, Lisa's spirit soared. With adrenaline surging through her, she felt an ember of something powerful within—hope mingled with fierce joy. She was not just running; she was fighting, claiming the life that was rightfully hers.

Trey regained his balance, his expression twisting into one of fury, but Lisa didn't wait to see what came next. She turned and fled deeper into the woods, her resolve an unbreakable shield that carried her forward, away from the darkness and into the promise of a new dawn.

Chapter Fourteen

The chill of the air did little to cool the fevered pace of events that had hurled Lisa into a life-or-death sprint. Just days ago, the quiet town and the forest had been a sanctuary; now, it was the stage for a harrowing game of survival. The image of Oliver, rugged and resolute, lying injured after trying to defend her from Trey's violent outburst, flickered in her mind. Lisa had never seen such malice in Trey's eyes before—not until he lunged at her with unmasked rage, forcing her to fight back with a desperation she didn't know she possessed.

Her escape had been narrow, a frantic dash into the embrace of the woods, where the twisted labyrinth of trees offered both concealment and peril. The forest, dense and untamed, swallowed her whole as if conspiring to hide her from her pursuer. Each breath was a gasp of icy air, each step an erratic drumbeat thudding against the earthy floor. Sharp and unyielding fear spurred her on, even as brambles clawed at her clothes and branches snagged her hair.

Lisa scanned the terrain through a filter of dread, registering every shadow and movement as a potential threat. The towering pines stood like silent sentinels, their needles whispering secrets of the wild as they brushed against one another. She could feel the dampness seeping through her sneakers, the soil beneath her becoming softer and more treacherous with each hurried stride.

The urgency that propelled her was palpable, a tangible force that mingled with the raw beauty of her surroundings. Moss-covered logs were not obstacles but vaults propelling her forward, while the thick underbrush became a friend, offering brief moments of cover. Her heart raced, a relentless tempo pushing her beyond what she thought possible, each beat a reminder of the danger that tore through the stillness behind her. Oliver, with his sea-tempered gaze, had always said she underestimated her own strength, and now that very strength was all that stood between her and the menacing chase of Trey's violent intent.

With every fiber of her being screaming for respite, Lisa pushed onward with the forest closing around her, a green haven laced with terror.

∼

Lisa pivoted sharply, her sneakers digging into the loamy earth as she ducked behind a broad oak. Her breath came in shallow bursts, each inhale an effort to silence the panic that urged her to reckless speed. The woods were a labyrinth of living green, and now, they were her lifeline. She allowed herself a split second to listen—only the muted hum of forest life greeted her ears before she was moving again.

She traced a path known only to the deer and the occasional daring hiker, her movements a silent dance with nature. There was a rhythm to her flight, a pattern learned from watching Oliver as he guided her through. Lisa's nimble form weaved between saplings, her dexterity belying the sense of peril that clung to her like a morning mist. Fallen logs, once seats for contemplation, became hurdles that she vaulted with a grace born of desperation.

The underbrush, thick with ferns and unseen life, brushed against her jeans as she plowed through it. She used it as a veil, crouching low and pausing to make herself as small as possible, hoping to blend with the natural tapestry. She could imagine Oliver's voice, strong yet soothing, encouraging her to stay smart and to use every advantage. He had taught her about these woods, and that knowledge was her shield, her compass.

But then, violating the sanctuary of whispering leaves and hidden birdsong, came the sound of pursuit. Trey's footsteps, heavy and determined, throbbed through the ground like a dark heartbeat.

As he drew nearer, his breathing became a grotesque symphony amid the stillness—a reminder that the hunter was closing in on the hunted.

Snap! A twig broke underfoot somewhere behind her, the sound sharp and accusing in the quiet wilderness. Lisa froze, her heart hammering against her ribs, every muscle tensed to flee. She didn't dare to look back—couldn't risk the precious seconds. Instead, she listened as the rustle of leaves betrayed his position—a predator weaving through the same foliage she had hoped would be her salvation.

With each crackling step he took, the illusion of safety shattered further, leaving her exposed among the towering trees that had once felt like allies. The forest held its breath, and so did she, before the unbearable tension broke, sending her surging forward once more, propelled by a will to survive that burned brighter than fear.

Trey's presence was a shadow that stretched with the waning light, a chilling reminder that no matter how fast she ran or how well she hid, he was relentless. But so was she. With every step, Lisa carried not just the hope of escape but the determination to reclaim the peace that had been stolen from her in those frantic, heart-stopping moments.

The soft loam beneath Lisa's sneakers gave way to a sprinter's rhythm, each stride an echo of the pulse racing through her veins. She dared a glance over her shoulder, and a jolt of terror shot through her—the gap between her and Trey had narrowed alarmingly, and he was holding out the gun. He fired a shot but didn't hit her. She could hear him curse behind her as he fired again. Lisa shrieked, then took a sharp turn as the bullet whistled past her back and hit the trunk of a tree beside her. Lisa felt panic as she knew Trey was going for another shot.

But this time, the gun clicked.

There were no more bullets.

Trey groaned loudly like a bear, then threw the gun after her. It landed in a pile of needles, and she continued, feeling a sliver of hope while Trey closed in on her. His face, a mask of grim determination, bore down on her with an intensity that belied his usually charming facade. Lisa's eyes, wide and reflecting the glimmers of coming daylight, betrayed her panic. Yet within that stark fear, a fierce determination took root, fueling her legs to push harder against the earth, her fight-or-flight response kicking into overdrive.

The forest became a blur of shadows and fleeting light as Lisa wove between trees, their bark rough under her palms as she used them for leverage. A fallen branch snagged at her ankle, threatening to send her tumbling, but she caught herself with a grace born of desperation. Behind her, Trey's footsteps grew thunderous, a relentless drumbeat in pursuit of its desperate prey.

In one heart-stopping moment, Lisa stumbled, her foot catching in a tangle of roots. She pitched forward, a silent scream lodged in her throat, but instinctively rolled to the side just as Trey lunged where she'd been moments before. Leaves and dirt flew up around him as he missed his grasp by mere inches.

Scrambling to her feet, Lisa didn't pause to relish the narrow escape. There was no time for relief, only the visceral need to survive. Each near-capture only heightened the tension winding tight within her chest, a spring coiled and ready to snap.

She darted to the left, barely avoiding a grasping hand that seemed to emerge from the encroaching darkness itself. Trey's breath was a hot gust on the back of her neck, and she could almost hear the smirk in his voice as he called out, "You can't run forever, Lisa!"

But she could run—she would run—her love for Oliver, her children, the small town that had become her sanctuary, and the lives that intertwined with hers propelled her onward. Her heart sang a silent promise with every stride: she would not let darkness claim her.

And so, Lisa ran, not just away from the threat behind her, but toward hope—a hope that beat in sync with the pounding of her heart, exciting and heartwarming even amidst the chase.

∼

Lisa's lungs burned with the effort of her escape, the cold air sharpening each breath as she plunged deeper into the woods. Her mind raced almost as fast as her feet, scrambling for a solution, a hiding spot, anything to evade Trey's relentless pursuit. The forest was an ally and adversary all at once, offering concealment but also obstacles that threatened to betray her presence with every snapped twig and rustled leaf.

Desperation lent her speed as she veered off the beaten track, leaves and mud flying beneath her frantic steps. She stumbled upon it, nearly invisible under the overgrowth: a narrow trail winding away like a lifeline through the dense foliage.

With Trey's heavy footsteps still echoing behind her, Lisa darted down the path, her heart soaring with a flicker of hope. She emerged into a small clearing dappled with moonlight that seemed to guide her to a brief sanctuary. Gasping for air, she pressed herself against the trunk of a massive oak, its ancient roots sprawling like guardians around her trembling form. Here, she allowed herself a moment —just one—to catch her breath and listen for any sign of her pursuer.

Meanwhile, Oliver's consciousness clawed its way back through the fog of pain that clouded his senses. His body protested every movement with jolts of agony from the injuries he'd sustained, yet his resolve remained unshaken. He pushed himself up from the ground, gritting his teeth against the searing protest of his battered ribs. The distant sounds of the chase—a woman's desperate flight, a man's hungry pursuit—reached his ears, igniting a fire within him that no injury could extinguish.

Oliver took a step, then another, each one a battle against the darkness that threatened to pull him under once more. His love for Lisa was guiding him through the pain. He leaned heavily on a fallen branch, repurposed into a makeshift crutch, and hobbled forward, following the cacophony of survival that pierced the otherwise tranquil night.

"Lisa," he murmured, the name both a prayer and a vow as he navigated the treacherous terrain. His vision swam with the effort, blurring the forest into a tapestry of shadows and moonlight, but he did not stop. He couldn't. Not when everything that mattered was slipping further into peril with each passing second. Oliver knew what he faced—a trial by earth and by blood—but the thought of Lisa alone with Trey spurred him onward, relentless as the tide.

Oliver's breath came in ragged gasps, each one etching lines of pain across his battered frame. The woods were a blur of darkness and danger, but his heart carried an image of Lisa that burned brighter than any fear. The urgency pulsing through him dulled each throb of anguish—a relentless drumbeat that whispered her name with every step.

No one knew these woods better than Oliver, and he soon found a shortcut leading to the old trail.

Ahead, the moonlight broke through the canopy, casting a silver glow on a scene that tightened Oliver's gut with dread. He saw Lisa first, her figure limned with desperation, darting glances over her shoulder where Trey loomed—a specter clothed in malice. Lisa's wavy hair was a wild cascade, tangled from her flight, and her eyes reflected a cocktail of terror and defiance.

"Lisa!" His voice was a hoarse shout, the sound tearing at his throat as he plunged into the clearing. Time seemed to contract around him, narrowing his world to this moment, to the promise he'd made to protect her, no matter the cost.

Trey turned at the sound, his eyes locking onto Oliver's with the cold calculation of a predator. A sneer twisted his lips as he measured the threat of an injured man.

"Playing hero again, Thompson?" he taunted, his voice a venomous drawl.

But Oliver's gaze remained steadfastly on Lisa, communicating a silent vow. *I'm here.* Together, they were more than their fears, more than the sum of past wounds. His approach was unsteady, each stride a battle against the darkness clawing at his conscious-ness, a testament to a love that refused to yield.

"Leave her alone, Trey," Oliver's words were laced with grit, his stance protective despite the tremor of pain that danced up his spine. His blue eyes, mirrors of the ocean's depths, never wavered from the threat before them.

Lisa's fear ebbed for a heartbeat, replaced by fierce gratitude as she witnessed Oliver's resolve. His presence was a fortress, a light of hope amidst the chaos. But as the seconds stretched taut, it was clear that a confrontation was inevitable—a clash under the watchful eyes of the whispering trees.

Oliver lunged forward, his body a mixture of coiled tension and sheer force as he collided with Trey. They crashed to the forest floor in a tangle of limbs, the impact jarring Oliver's already injured frame. But pain was a distant echo against the adrenaline that surged through his veins.

Trey snarled beneath him, his rage palpable as he bucked wildly, attempting to throw Oliver off. But Oliver had weathered storms fiercer than the man before him; his hands found purchase on Trey's wrists, pinning them to the ground with the vise-like grip borne from hauling nets and battling the unforgiving sea.

"Enough, Trey!" Oliver barked, each word punctuated by the raw determination etched into his features. His eyes were stormy seas now, reflecting a tempest of protective ferocity.

Lisa watched, frozen, her chest heaving with ragged breaths as the two men grappled for supremacy. The sight of Oliver battered yet unyielding, swelled within her a tide of mingled emotions. Despite her terror, a spark of awe ignited in her gaze, witnessing the lengths to which he'd go to shield her from harm.

Trey bucked again, a wildcat cornered and desperate, but Oliver anticipated his movements. With a fisherman's innate sense of the current, he shifted his weight, pressing down harder, an immovable object against the frenzied assault.

"Stop," Lisa found her voice amidst the chaos, the single word slicing through the fray like a beacon of sanity. Her plea seemed to lend Oliver added strength, and he redoubled his efforts, subduing Trey with a grunt of exertion.

Finally, as the struggle reached its crescendo, Oliver's resilience won out. He twisted Trey's arm behind his back sharply, eliciting a yelp of pain from the man who, seconds ago, had been the embodiment of menace. Panting heavily and wincing in pain, Oliver secured Trey's other arm, rendering him powerless, his face pressed into the loamy soil.

"Lisa, call for help," Oliver managed to say, his voice a hoarse whisper strained by effort and injury.

As she scrambled to her feet, her fingers fumbling for her phone, relief began to wash over Lisa in warm waves as she realized there was actually a connection this deep in the woods. She dialed with shaking hands, then relayed their location to the authorities, praying they would be able to find them. All the while, her eyes never left the scene before her—Oliver's steadfast form ensuring Trey could inflict no more damage.

"Help is on the way, ma'am. Just stay with me," the operator's voice crackled through the phone, each word slicing through the haze of Lisa's fear like a lighthouse piercing the fog.

A sigh escaped her lips—a whisper of relief as the promise of aid weaved its way into the fabric of the tumultuous night. She watched, her heart a symphony of gratitude and hope, as Oliver maintained his hold over Trey. His shoulders rose and fell with the exertion, his strength a testament to the love that fueled him.

"Thank you," Lisa breathed into the receiver, her gaze never leaving Oliver. She could see the strain in his posture, the tremble in his arms from the weight of the struggle. Yet, he was an unbreakable chain, a guardian between her and the chaos Trey had brought upon them.

Oliver's jaw was set, his eyes—deep as the ocean whence he came—flashing with the fire of a man who had weathered many storms. This one, however fierce, would not best him. The muscles in his forearms bulged as he adjusted his grip on Trey, ensuring there was no escape for the man beneath him.

"Almost over," Oliver murmured, half to himself, half to Lisa. He knew the stakes; he wasn't just fighting for justice but for a future free from the shadows that Trey cast over their lives.

Lisa wrapped her free arm around herself, comforted by the connection still alive on the other end of the line. The operator's voice was now the rhythm keeping her grounded as she stood sentinel over the two men entwined on the ground.

The minutes stretched on, each one a brushstroke painting the end of this ordeal. And there, under the silver gaze of the moon, Lisa saw it—the shimmering thread of a new beginning, woven through the grit and resolve of the man who held her heart. Battered yet unbowed, Oliver was the promise of dawn after the longest night.

She knelt beside Oliver, her hand trembling as it brushed his cheek, a silent gesture laden with the depth of her gratitude.

"Thank you."

Oliver's answering smile was pained but genuine, a harbinger of solace amidst the turmoil.

"Always, Lisa."

Gravel dug into Oliver's forearms as he fought to maintain his hold on Trey. Every sinew in his body tensed, fibers burning with exertion as if they were cords being pulled taut in a game of tug-of-war. His breath came out in ragged gasps, hot against the chill of the Alaskan evening air. His heart raced, each pulse a drumbeat that echoed his singular resolve to keep Lisa safe.

Trey bucked beneath him, a wild animal caught in a trap, his movements sharp and desperate. But Oliver was an anchor in the midst of a storm, his arms unwavering despite the strain that screamed through his limbs. The knowledge that it wasn't just his own well-being at stake here but Lisa's future—their future—fueled him with a strength that seemed drawn from the very depths of his soul.

Trey was screaming and squirming beneath him, trying to get him off. He rolled sideways and managed to kick Oliver in the stomach, which resulted in Oliver slamming his fist into his face and knocking him out. Panting, Oliver stood to his feet, and Lisa grabbed him in her arms just as he fell to his knees.

As they waited for the sirens to pierce the silence of the woods, shared understanding passed between them. In the aftermath of terror, an undeniable bond was forged in the crucible of their ordeal—a connection that transcended fear and spoke of a far more profound emotion.

Lisa's heart raced still, but now it beat to a different rhythm—one filled with the promise of safety and the hint of something new awakening between them. Oliver's protective embrace was both a refuge and a revelation, the warmth of it seeping into her bones, chasing away the cold dread that had gripped her.

And in the quiet of the forest, with danger subdued and hearts laid bare, it was clear that this moment would be etched into the very fabric of their being, a testament to courage, sacrifice, and the unexpected gift of love growing in the shadow of peril.

The forest's symphony of life tentatively resumed, a whispering backdrop to the heavy breaths that shuddered from Lisa and Oliver. They sat, backs against the coarse bark of an ancient fir, their fingers entwined—a small lifeline in the vast sea of green. Lisa's gaze wandered over Oliver's face, noting the bruises blooming like dark flowers under his skin, the blood that traced a path down his sweater from his shoulder where the bullet had hit.

"Are you okay?" Her voice cracked on the words, each syllable laden with concern and a weariness that seemed to settle in her very bones.

Oliver winced as he shifted, a grimace cutting through the stoic facade he had erected.

"I'll live," he murmured. But his eyes, those deep blue wells of determination, betrayed the pain he felt, the effort it took to stitch a smile onto his lips for her sake.

Lisa's heart swelled, even as it ached. Here was a man who, despite his own injuries, had risen like some mythic guardian from the cold embrace of unconsciousness to stand between her and certain doom. His bravery wrapped around her, as tangible as the arm he now draped over her shoulders, pulling her closer.

Yet, as the adrenaline that had fueled her flight began to ebb, Lisa felt the tremors of reality shake the foundation of the moment. The danger had passed, but at what cost? She could see the toll etched into Oliver's exhausted features, feel it in the way his body subtly recoiled from her touch where bruises lay hidden beneath his shirt.

Their shared silence spoke volumes; each unvoiced thought a weight that threatened to fracture the fragile peace they'd found. As she rested her head against his other shoulder, the uncertainty of the future loomed large, an invisible specter among the trees.

"Where do we go from here, Oliver?" Lisa whispered, her words barely audible above the rustling leaves.

He turned to her, eyes searching, and for a heartbeat, the world held its breath. "Together," he said simply. And in that single word, there was a vow, a silent promise that whatever storms may come, they would weather them side by side.

But as the distant wail of sirens finally shattered the quiet of the forest, signaling the arrival of help, another sound—a faint, chilling howl—rose from the depths of the woods as Trey woke up. Oliver stiffened, and Lisa's pulse quickened anew.

"Oliver," she started, but he hushed her with a finger to her lips. Then he went and sat on top of Trey's back with a smile while the sirens filled the air around them, and they began to hear voices approach.

"We got this," he assured her, though his gaze

remained locked on the body below him from which the howl had emanated.

A few feet away, rooted to the spot on the damp earth, stood Lisa. Sunlight glinted off her wavy hair, turning it into a halo of soft shadows around her pale face. Her lips parted slightly, a silent prayer escaping them as she watched the two men before her locked in this dance of survival. Tears brimmed in her eyes, not entirely born of fear but also of awe—at the sight of Oliver's relentless determination, at the sheer magnitude of his love that now displayed itself in every grueling twist and turn of his body.

Her hands clasped together, knuckles white, Lisa's gaze never wavered from Oliver. She saw beyond the violence of the moment, glimpsing the gentle spirit of the man who had shown her kindness when she'd least expected it, who had listened when she needed it most. And now, as morning light enveloped them, she saw the hero he'd become, willing to face down her demons so that she might never have to do so alone again.

Chapter Fifteen

The wail of sirens cleaved through the night, drawing nearer with each desperate beat of Oliver's heart. A symphony of relief and triumph swelled within him as the red and blue lights danced across the darkened trees like erratic fireflies signaling safety. The grip around Trey's wrists was no longer just a restraint; it was a bridge to the life he and Lisa deserved, away from the terror that had haunted their every step.

"Lisa," he called out, voice ragged but laced with a fervor that only raw emotion could forge. "They're coming."

Her response was not in words but in action—a rush of movement as she closed the distance between them. Her knees buckled on the cold grass beside Oliver, her arms encircling his broad shoulders with an intensity that matched the chaos of their ordeal. Lisa's body shook against him, a silent sob trapped behind the dam of her lips, her breath warm against his neck.

Oliver felt it then, the full weight of what they'd been through, the danger they'd narrowly skirted colliding with the sanctuary of the moment. His own body trembled, not with fear, but with the adrenaline that had fueled his fight now ebbing away like the tide returning to the sea. He allowed himself to feel it all—the pain from the wound in his shoulder, the fear, the hope—knowing they were on the precipice of something new.

As the police cruisers skidded to a stop and officers poured out, their shadows long in the flashing lights, Oliver finally eased his hold on Trey. He looked up at Lisa, her eyes reflecting the spinning lights that promised an end to the nightmare. In those eyes, he saw everything: the storm they'd weathered, the peace that lay ahead, and the unspoken promise that they would rebuild from the wreckage together.

"I love you," she whispered, her voice barely audible over the din of the arriving law enforcement. But Oliver heard her—felt her gratitude resonate within him, warming him against the chill of the night.

"I love you too," he replied, his tone steady and sure.

⁓

Oliver's grip on Trey loosened as the first officer reached them, his uniform a stark contrast against the dark backdrop of the mountains. Firm hands in blue took hold of Trey, pulling him from Oliver's exhausted clasp. The clamor of handcuffs closing around wrists sounded like victory, and with it, the weight of fear lifted.

"Stand back, sir," an officer directed, but Oliver heard it as if through water, his senses still buzzing from the confrontation.

"Oliver?" Lisa's voice anchored him back to reality, her hand reaching out to brush against his. He turned to look at her, their eyes meeting in a silent conversation that spoke volumes more than words ever could.

In the blue wash of the police lights, Oliver saw the remnants of terror fading from Lisa's face, replaced by a dawning hope. Her lips quivered into a smile that had been absent too long, its return a testament to the resilience within her. His heart, which had been thundering like stormy waves against a rocky shore, began to find a new rhythm—one of quiet strength and shared solace.

"We did it, Lisa. It's over," Oliver said, the words both a declaration and a promise.

"Thanks to you," she replied, her voice steady now, imbued with a newfound steadiness that mirrored the calm after a storm. "Guess you are a hero after all."

Around them, officers were securing the scene,

their radios crackling with updates and affirmations of safety restored. But in the small bubble where Lisa and Oliver stood, the chaos receded, leaving behind only two souls whose bond had been forged stronger in the fires of adversity.

Their hands found each other, fingers intertwining naturally as if they were two parts of a whole coming together after a long separation. The touch was grounding, a tangible sign of the life they could now rebuild, free from the shadows that had chased them.

Even amidst the flashing lights and the officers' movements, a sense of serenity settled over them. They had faced down the darkness, and in doing so, they had illuminated the path forward—a path they would walk together.

"Let's go home," Oliver murmured, already envisioning the comforting embrace of normalcy, the simple pleasures they could now enjoy without the specter of danger lurking nearby.

"Home, yes," Lisa echoed, the word blooming with possibilities and a future they were both eager to embrace. "But first, we need to get you to the hospital. I can see the ambulance; come with me."

Oliver marveled at her strength and grace in weathering this storm. Then, with a rush of warmth flooding his chest, he realized this was just the beginning of their story—one filled with the thrill of survival and the tender promise of love.

Chapter Sixteen

The dusty pickup truck's tires crunched over the gravel as it rolled to a stop on Main Street. Lisa's hand hovered above the door handle, her pulse thrumming with a cocktail of nerves and anticipation. With a deep breath that did little to steady her fluttering heart, she swung the door open, and the crisp air of the Alaskan town greeted her like an old friend.

"Here we go," Oliver said, his voice a warm balm against the chill. He stepped out, stretching his arms high above his head, his dark hair tousled by the wind. His eyes caught hers, reflecting the same mixture of relief and happiness that coursed through her.

Lisa followed suit, her boots making soft indentations in the snow-dusted ground. She couldn't help but marvel at the sight before her—the rugged mountains standing sentinel in the distance, the quaint homes with their puffing chimneys, and the local businesses adorned with welcome signs that seemed to have been hung just for them.

A ripple of excited murmurs washed over the gathering crowd as Lisa and Oliver's presence registered. The townspeople, bundled up in their winter best, began to approach with smiles that could melt glaciers. There was no hesitation, no judgment—just the unspoken language of acceptance weaving through the brisk air. The stories of their endeavors in the woods, fighting for their lives, and capturing Trey had run before them, and all knew what they had been through.

"Welcome back, Lisa!" called out a familiar voice. It was Mrs. Henderson.

"Oliver! Good to see ya home, son," boomed Mr. Jacobs, the hardware store owner, his wide grin splitting his weathered face.

"Thank you, everyone," Lisa managed, her voice barely above a whisper, but it didn't matter. The warmth in their eyes told her they heard her loud and clear.

Children darted between legs, dogs wagged their tails fervently, and laughter echoed off the storefronts. Each person who pressed forward to shake their hands or offer a hug only solidified the reality that this wasn't just a place; it was their place. Home.

"Never doubted you'd come back to us," chuckled Nancy, the innkeeper, her rosy cheeks lifted high with delight.

"Look at you two!" teased Bill, the town's mechanic, his thumbs hooked into his suspenders. "Makin' quite the pair!"

Their support swaddled Lisa in a quilt of communal love, something she hadn't realized she'd missed until now. And Oliver, ever the pillar beside her, shared in the collective joy, his hand finding its way to the small of her back, grounding her.

As the crowd enveloped them in celebratory chatter, Lisa allowed herself a moment to truly take it all in. Relief flooded her veins while happiness danced in her chest—a symphony of emotions playing to the tune of this heartwarming homecoming.

Amidst the gentle hum of reacquaintance, Lisa caught Oliver's eye, and a silent conversation passed between them—a shared recognition of the love that surrounded them. It was as though the vast Alaskan sky had opened up, pouring down a golden light that bathed them in its glow. Their hands brushed against each other, fingers tentatively intertwining, anchoring them to this moment.

The murmur of conversations softened as Maggie made her way through the crowd, her fiery curls a bright light amidst the sea of townsfolk. The lines on her face, usually animated with laughter or stern with concern, now relaxed into an expression of sheer relief and joy. Her eyes, rimmed with moisture, locked onto Lisa, reflecting decades of storms weathered and sunny days embraced.

"Lisa, my dear," Maggie breathed, her voice carrying the tremble of raw emotion. She enveloped Lisa in an embrace, the kind that spoke volumes more than words could ever convey.

The town watched, holding their collective breath, as Maggie held Lisa close, her shoulders shaking just slightly.

"We've missed you, girl," she said, her voice thick. The bar hadn't been the same without Lisa's quiet strength behind it, without her tender smiles that somehow made a shot of whiskey taste like a drop of pure comfort.

"Thank you, Maggie," Lisa replied, her voice muffled in the fabric of Maggie's sweater. "It feels so good to be back." She pulled back just enough to meet Maggie's gaze, and in those hazel eyes, Maggie saw not only the woman who had left but also the one who had returned—stronger, surer, and still every bit as much a part of this wild, loving community.

Standing by, Oliver gave Maggie an appreciative nod, his heart expanding as he witnessed the genuine affection these hardy souls reserved for one another. He knew then that the roots they were putting down here, together, were entwining with something much larger than themselves. This was a place where hardships were shared, joys were multiplied, and no one stood alone; this was home.

As Maggie finally released Lisa from the hug, she

turned to Oliver, offering him a knowing smile—one that said she understood the depth of what was unfolding before her very eyes. Oliver smiled back, his eyes sparkling with the promise of tomorrow. Together, they faced the crowd, ready to step forward into their shared future, with the blessing of the entire town warming them like the midsummer sun.

The crowd parted, and a mountain of a man emerged from the throng. Mark's shaved head caught the glint of the setting sun as he made his way toward Oliver with deliberate steps that seemed to shake the earth beneath them. His broad smile was a flare of rough affection in the sea of faces, and as he approached, Lisa felt Oliver's hand tighten around hers.

"Oliver, my man!" bellowed Mark, his voice rich and deep like the ocean they both knew so well. He engulfed Oliver in a bear hug that lifted him slightly off the ground. When they parted, he clapped Oliver's back with a force that would've felled a lesser man. "Welcome home, brother. This place hasn't been the same without you."

"Good to see you, Mark," Oliver replied, his grin mirroring the lumberjack's joy. "I'm counting on you to get me back into the swing of things."

"Say no more," Mark assured, his eyes twinkling. "You'll have your sea legs back before you know it, and I'm here for anything else you two need."

Lisa watched the exchange, her heart lifting further. The support emanating from everyone gathered filled her with a warmth that pushed away the last remnants of any lingering doubts she had about their return. These were people who held each other up; this was a community where love was action.

Before she could fully process the moment, another familiar figure wove through the crowd, her short black hair a stark contrast against the lighter shades surrounding her. Sarah's freckled face was alight with excitement, and when she reached Lisa, her arms opened wide.

"Lisa!" she exclaimed, embracing her former coworker enthusiastically. "The bar has been way too quiet without your laughter echoing behind the counter. We all missed your stories, your smiles, everything!"

"Sarah, it's so wonderful to see you," Lisa said, her voice tinged with emotion as she returned the tight hug. She pulled back to look at the young woman's radiant face, feeling the genuine happiness that Sarah exuded. It made Lisa's smile grow wider and her spirit lighter.

"Can't wait to catch up over a shift together," Sarah continued, her bubbly energy undiminished. "It's going to be just like old times, but even better!"

"Definitely better," Lisa agreed, her gaze drifting over to Oliver, who was now laughing at another of Mark's jokes. The future seemed to beckon them with open arms, and the promise of those better days shone brightly in their friends' faces, new and old.

As the Alaskan twilight began to stretch its colors across the sky, painting the town in hues of pink and gold, Lisa and Oliver stood surrounded by the people who made this place more than just a dot on the map. It was a haven of shared lives and intertwined destinies—a place where they could weave their own tale into the fabric of the community, secure in the knowledge that they were exactly where they were meant to be.

As Lisa and Oliver mingled with the townsfolk, an impromptu circle formed around a crackling fire pit just outside Maggie's local bar. The orange glow flickered across familiar faces as everyone settled into worn lawn chairs, their breaths visible in the cool Alaskan air. It was a tradition for stories to be shared here, but tonight, the tales woven had a special warmth to them.

"Remember when the Henderson's barn got hit by that big storm?" began Pete, the town's elder statesman, his voice rich with the timbre of age and wisdom. "We all thought it'd be a goner, but not a soul hesitated. We were up at the crack of dawn, hammers in hand."

Lisa watched as heads nodded, smiles spreading in remembrance of collective effort and triumph.

Oliver squeezed her hand gently, his eyes reflecting the firelight and his pride for his hometown.

"Couldn't let those cows go without shelter," chimed in Janet, who ran the general store, her usually stern face softened by the camaraderie. "Took us two days straight, but we did it. That's what neighbors are for."

The crowd murmured their agreement, the bonds of shared hardship and solidarity evident in every syllable. Lisa felt something inside her unfurl—a tightness she hadn't realized she'd been carrying. She sensed the depth of community spirit here, surrounded by these resilient souls. It wasn't just about survival; it was about thriving together.

"Or the time little Timmy got lost in the woods," added Sarah, her voice tinged with laughter. "Half the town turned out to search. Found him napping under a spruce, snug as could be."

"Scared us half to death," Mark boomed from beside Oliver, "but it showed us all just how much we look out for each other's kin."

Lisa glanced up at Oliver, seeing the embodiment of this place in him—its steadfastness, care, and the unspoken promise to hold you up when you might falter. As each story unfurled, a tapestry of interwoven lives and shared experiences, she knew they were threads in this fabric, too.

"Feels like we're part of something special, doesn't it?" Oliver whispered, his breath warm against her ear.

"More than special," Lisa responded, her voice barely above a murmur yet carrying the weight of revelation. "It feels like home, our home."

The fire crackled merrily as if in approval, and the night sky stretched vast and clear above them, a canopy of stars witnessing the silent pledge of two hearts finding their harbor. In the warmth of the fire and the strength of the arms encircling her, Lisa knew that no matter how far they wandered, this small Alaskan town, with its towering pines and indomitable spirit, would always call them back. It was here, among these enduring friendships and the promise of new beginnings, that they had found a place where love and belonging converged, welcoming them into its fold with open arms and endless skies. There was only one thing missing for Lisa to make her life perfect, and even that Maggie had made sure to take care of.

The crackle of the fire had faded into a distant memory as Lisa's gaze found the two figures darting through the gathering crowd. Maggie stood proudly behind them, smiling from ear to ear.

"I believe these two belong to you," she said. "The sheriff brought them here from Seattle while you two were spending your days in the hospital recovering."

Abigail's curly hair bounced like a spring lamb's

first leap, and Ethan advanced with a quiet determination that belied his tender years. Their faces were radiant in the twilight, reflecting a joy so pure it cut through the evening chill.

"Mommy!" Abigail's voice pierced the cool Alaskan air, a triumphant chirp that beckoned every eye toward the unfolding moment.

Ethan, less vocal but no less enthused, sprinted silently, his hazel eyes locked onto his mother. They moved in unison, a dual force propelled by longing and love, unstoppable in their quest to bridge the gap that time and distance had imposed upon them.

As they reached her, Lisa dropped to her knees, her arms opening wide to welcome the onrush of small bodies. Abigail collided with her in a whirlwind of giggles and chatter while Ethan wrapped his arms around them both, grounding the trio in a silent embrace that spoke volumes of the days they'd spent apart. She held them close, feeling the rapid beat of their young hearts against her own, an echo of a rhythm that spelled "home" in its purest form.

"Everything's going to be okay now," Lisa murmured into Abigail's ear, then kissed Ethan's forehead, her words less for them and more a promise to herself.

A little distance away, Oliver stood witness to this tender reunion, a soft smile gracing his lips. His eyes brimmed with emotion, and he felt a surge of protectiveness, a desire to preserve the sanctity of this moment. He saw not just Lisa or her children but a constellation of souls coming together, a family unit being reborn before his very eyes.

Abigail, ever the explorer, pulled back first, her mischievous smile aimed up at Oliver.

"Are you going to join the hug, Oliver?" she asked, her innocence wrapping around the question like a warm blanket. "Mommy's told us everything about you on the phone."

Oliver stepped forward and knelt beside them with a chuckle that rumbled from deep within.

"I thought you'd never ask," he said, and his arms encircled the family, drawing them all into a new circle of comfort. In that instant, his heart committed to whatever future lay ahead, to the laughter and the challenges, to the quiet nights and stormy days. This was his harbor, too, and these were the souls he'd cast his lot with.

Abigail and Ethan, nestled between their mother and Oliver, giggled and squirmed happily in the shared space. The warmth from their bodies mingled with the love in the air, crafting an electric current that hummed through the group.

They were a portrait of unity—a mother, her children, and the man who had become part of their story. And beneath the early stars beginning to twinkle in the Alaskan sky, Oliver knew without a doubt that they had indeed found a new family in this small town. Here, where the mountains stood guard and the rivers sang lullabies, they would forge their path together, bound not just by affection but by the collective embrace of a community that had claimed them all as its own.

Laughter and the clinking of dishes filled the air as Lisa and Oliver entered Maggie's tavern. The scent of baked salmon and berry cobbler wove through the room, a gustatory welcome from the town that had watched over them with silent strength. Tables adorned with handmade quilts and flickering candles beckoned them further into the heartwarming embrace of their neighbors.

"Welcome home, once again. We thought we'd give you a big welcome, and what's a better welcome than food?" said Maggie, coming up with a steaming pot of stew, her eyes glistening with unshed tears. Mark was right beside her, his large hands balancing a tray laden with fresh bread and butter. The townspeople followed suit, their offerings of food and smiles laid out like a feast not just for the body but for weary souls too.

Lisa's eyes sparkled with unspoken emotion as she took in the scene. The room buzzed with a vibrant energy that seemed to pulse directly from the heart of the community. She let out a soft, disbelieving laugh, her hand finding Oliver's, their fingers weaving together as naturally as the rivers meet the sea.

"Can you believe this?" she whispered, her voice barely audible over the din of friendly chatter.

Oliver squeezed her hand gently, the roughness of his fisherman's grip a comforting contrast to hers.

"They're family," he replied, his eyes reflecting the candlelight and the sincerity of his words.

The evening unfurled like a well-loved storybook; each page turned to bring another heartfelt conversation, another shared memory. Plates were piled high, and laughter came easily. The warmth within the tavern rivaled even that of the summer sun, which refused to dip below the horizon.

As the night wound down and the mountains outside cast long shadows across the wooden floor, Lisa and Oliver found themselves standing slightly apart from the crowd. Their hands remained intertwined, the thrumming gratitude between them spilling over into the space they occupied.

"Look at them all," Lisa murmured, her gaze sweeping across the faces illuminated by the soft glow of the center's lights. "This is more than I ever hoped for."

"More than we both did," Oliver agreed, his arm slipping around her waist to draw her closer. In the shelter of his embrace, Lisa allowed herself to relax and truly take in the depth of what they had been given—a second chance wrapped in the unconditional support of an entire town.

"Thank you," she breathed out, though she wasn't sure whether it was to Oliver, the townspeople, or some unseen force that had guided her back here. But it didn't matter. The sentiment was felt deeply, a shared sentiment that needed no elaboration.

"Let's never take this for granted," Oliver said, his voice holding a solemn vow that resonated with every beat of Lisa's heart.

"Never," she echoed, her head resting against his chest, listening to the steady rhythm that promised tomorrow and all the days after. Together, they stood in silent reverence for the precious tapestry of moments that had woven them into the fabric of this small Alaskan town—a tapestry rich with love and newfound hope.

Oliver reached for Lisa's hand, his fingers interlacing with hers in a firm yet gentle grip. The soft buzz of conversation from the departing towns-people faded into the background as they shared a look that went beyond words. Their eyes—hazel meeting ocean blue—held a silent promise, an unspoken pact that resonated with the clarity of the crisp Alaskan air.

They stepped out into the cool night, leaving the warmth of the tavern behind. The stars overhead shimmered like a celestial tapestry, their brilliance reflecting the sparkle that danced in Lisa's gaze. She squeezed Oliver's hand, feeling the roughness of his calluses, badges of his life as a fisherman, and now, symbols of their intertwined lives. The kids walked behind them, giggling playfully.

A light breeze whisked past them, carrying the scent of pine and the distant murmur of the sea. They moved through the quiet streets, each step a beat in the rhythm of their shared journey. The wooden storefronts and cozy homes stood as silent sentinels, witnesses to the beginning of their new chapter.

"Can you believe it?" Lisa's voice was barely above a whisper, her breath forming small clouds that hung in the air before dissipating.

"Believe it? I'm counting on it," Oliver said, his tone laced with the same resolve he used to brave the tempestuous waves. "This place, these people... we're part of something special here."

Lisa nodded, feeling the weight of her past loosening its grip with every footfall on the familiar gravel roads. Here, in this remote corner of the world, she had found more than she had ever dared to dream—a community, a partner, a haven.

They all paused by the edge of the water, where the town met the endless expanse of the ocean. The moon cast a silver path across the surface, beckoning them toward tomorrow's promise. They looked at each other, their shared understanding deepening.

"Home," Lisa said simply, the word encapsulating the enormity of their emotions. She put her arms around both children's shoulders and pulled them close.

"Home," Oliver echoed, his smile reflecting both contentment and excitement for what lay ahead.

Hand in hand, they continued their walk, the future calling to them with every heartwarming echo of laughter that spilled from houses and the exciting possibilities whispered by the wind. In this small Alaskan town, Lisa and Oliver had discovered a love that would endure the harshest winters and bloom with the coming of each spring—a love as vast and enduring as the landscape that cradled it.

Chapter Seventeen

Lisa flitted from one room to the other, her hands fluttering over the freshly made beds topped with quilts sewn with patterns of bears and moose. She arranged a stack of storybooks on Abigail's nightstand, each tale brimming with Alaskan wilderness adventures. She placed a model fishing boat on Ethan's shelf, imagining his fingers tracing its miniature lines.

"Look at this, Oliver," she said, stepping back to admire the setup, her eyes reflecting a mix of anticipation and tender care. "Do you think they'll like it?"

Standing in the doorway with his arms crossed, Oliver watched her with an affectionate grin. He had asked them all to move in with him in his house. He walked over and gently wrapped an arm around her shoulders. "They're going to love it," he assured her, his voice steady as the roll of distant ocean waves. "You've outdone yourself, Lisa."

"First thing tomorrow, we'll show them the creek behind the house," Lisa suggested, her voice tinged with excitement. "Abigail can chase dragonflies, and Ethan... maybe he'll enjoy just sitting by the water, you know? It's so peaceful."

"Perfect," Oliver agreed, nodding, his eyes lighting up at the thought.

The sound of tires crunching on gravel outside sent a surge of energy through the house. Lisa's heart skipped a beat as she exchanged a knowing look with Oliver. This was it. Abigail and Ethan were here. Maggie had promised to bring them to their new home after taking them for breakfast at the local diner and then back-to-school shopping so Lisa and Oliver could have the time to prepare their rooms. They had all stayed at the inn for a few days while Lisa got everything ready.

Rushing to the front door, they swung it open to the crisp air, the late afternoon sun casting golden hues across the porch. Two small figures emerged from the car, their faces a canvas of mixed emotions— curiosity painting their expressions as they took in their new home.

"Mom! Oliver!" Abigail's voice cut through the quiet, her curly hair bouncing as she ran into Lisa's waiting arms.

"Hey, sport," Oliver ruffled Ethan's blond hair as he approached more cautiously. His young face was serious, but his eyes held a glint of wonder.

"Welcome home, my loves," Lisa whispered,

embracing them both, her voice soft yet resonating with a strength born from past trials. "Everything's going to be alright now."

"Let us show you inside," Oliver said, taking each child's hand in his own, his touch reassuring.

They guided the children through the threshold, pointing out the hooks by the door where their coats would hang, the fireplace that would keep them warm during winter nights, and the cozy nook by the window that was perfect for reading or dreaming.

"Your rooms are upstairs," Lisa led the way, her voice laced with warmth. "We wanted you to have your own special places."

Abigail's room greeted her with walls adorned with a mural of a serene forest, complete with hidden creatures for her to discover. She squealed with delight, darting from corner to corner as her imagination took flight.

Ethan's room was a quiet harbor, shades of blue reflecting the calm of the sea. A telescope pointed toward the curtain-draped window promised starry explorations and his gaze lingered on the intricate fishing boat, a silent acknowledgment of this new chapter.

"Mom," Ethan murmured, the beginning of a smile tugging at his lips, "it's really nice."

"Thank you," Abigail chimed in, wrapping her arms around Lisa in a tight hug.

"Anything for you two," Lisa replied, her eyes misty with happiness as she looked over at Oliver.

Together, they shared a silent promise, one filled with hope and the joy of family finally reunited.

The sun had barely climbed above the horizon when Lisa and Oliver, hand in hand with Abigail and Ethan, stepped outside the next morning. A thin layer of dew shimmered on the grass, and the sky blushed with the early hues of dawn.

"Welcome to your first Alaskan adventure," Oliver announced with a grin as wide as the river they were about to explore. His eyes were alight with excitement, reflecting the promise of the day ahead.

Abigail skipped ahead; the allure of the unknown swept away her earlier apprehension.

"Are we going to see bears?" she asked, her voice bubbling with curiosity.

"Maybe," Lisa said, winking at Ethan, who walked cautiously at her side. "But we'll be safe. Oliver knows these parts like the back of his hand."

They trekked through the whispering pines, the scent of spruce tickling their senses. Every so often, Oliver would pause to point out tracks imprinted in the soft earth or to explain the calls of distant birds. Abigail listened intently, cataloging each detail in her vibrant imagination, while Ethan absorbed the information quietly, his eyes scanning the wilderness with a serene intensity.

"Look!" Abigail squealed, pointing toward the

riverbank where a moose and her calf grazed peacefully. They all watched in silent wonder, sharing a moment of connection not just to each other but to the pulse of life around them.

Hours later, as the afternoon sun cast long shadows over the house, the family found themselves gathered in the kitchen, surrounded by the aroma of cooking salmon and the warmth from the oven.

"Salmon is a staple here," Oliver explained as he carefully showed Ethan how to season the fillets. "It's about respecting what the land and sea provide for us."

Ethan nodded, his concentration etched in the careful way he mimicked Oliver's movements. Meanwhile, Lisa and Abigail were at the counter, laughter spilling from them like sunlight as they mixed ingredients for a berry cobbler.

"Alaska has some of the best berries you'll ever taste," Lisa told her daughter, guiding her hand as they poured the ruby-red mixture into a baking dish.

"Can we pick our own berries sometime?" Abigail asked, her face hopeful.

"Of course, sweetheart," Lisa assured her, tucking a stray curl behind Abigail's ear. "We'll make it another adventure."

As the meal came together, the house was filled with more than just the scents of dinner—it was awash with the sounds and sensations of four people weaving a new tapestry of memories. They shared tales of past excursions, dreams of the future, and the simple pleasure of the present.

When they finally sat down to eat, the table was a portrait of togetherness—a feast lovingly prepared and eagerly shared. Each flavor was a testament to the land that now embraced them, and every laugh was a stitch in the fabric of their growing bond.

"Here's to new beginnings," Oliver toasted, raising his glass to the light dancing off the walls.

"New beginnings," Lisa echoed, her gaze lingering on the faces of her children—their smiles a reflection of her own.

"To Alaska," Abigail chimed in, her eyes sparkling with mischief and merriment.

"And to family," Ethan added softly, his voice steady and sure.

Their glasses clinked in a chorus of hope, the sound echoing through the house and into the heart of the wilderness beyond.

The crackling fire cast a cozy glow across the living room as Lisa and Oliver settled onto the couch with Abigail and Ethan nestled between them. Outside, the twilight lingered, painting the sky in hues of purples and blues, a silent witness to the intimate moment unfolding within.

"Mom," Ethan's voice was hesitant, his eyes tracing the knots in the wooden floor before daring to meet hers. "Back at home... Dad used to be really mean to me. He would sometimes hit me... hit the both of us."

Lisa's heart clenched at the vulnerability of her son's confession. She reached out, gently tilting his chin so he could see the sincerity in her gaze. "I'm sorry you went through that, Ethan. But you're incredibly strong, you know that?"

Beside him, Abigail fidgeted, her small hands wringing the hem of her shirt. "It was scary when we had to leave home so fast. Will we have to do that again?"

Oliver wrapped an arm around each child, pulling them close. His eyes, usually reflecting the vast ocean, now held a storm of protection and care.

"You're safe here with us. Alaska is your fortress, and we're not going anywhere," Lisa said.

"Your mother and I, we've faced some rough seas ourselves," Oliver said, casting a glance at Lisa. "We've learned that sometimes the wind blows you off course to take you to where you truly belong."

"Like here?" Abigail's voice was small but curious.

"Exactly like here," Lisa smiled, kissing the top of her daughter's head. "And now, we'll find our way together."

"Speaking of finding our way," Oliver chimed in, his tone shifting to playful conspiration, "I think it's time we create some new traditions."

"Traditions?" Ethan's curiosity was piqued, a faint smile beginning to form.

"Every family needs them," Lisa said. "They're like anchors in a storm. They keep us connected."

"Movie marathons, game nights, exploring trails," Oliver began to list, watching the children's faces light up with each suggestion. "And every Saturday morning, we'll chart our own course—whether fishing, berry picking, or just watching the sunrise."

"Can we make s'mores?" Abigail asked.

"Absolutely," Lisa laughed. "S'mores are mandatory."

"Will there be stars?" Ethan wondered aloud, his imagination already reaching for the constellations hidden by daylight.

"More stars than you can count," Oliver assured him, his voice steady as the tides.

"Sounds perfect," Ethan murmured, leaning back against the cushions, his previous fears ebbing away with each shared plan.

"Perfect," Abigail echoed, her eyelids heavy with contentment as she snuggled deeper into the safety of her family's embrace.

As the fire dwindled to embers, the cabin hummed with the energy of new beginnings and the quiet strength of a family united. Tomorrow would bring its own adventures, but tonight, they reveled in the simple joy of belonging. In the heart of Alaska, under a blanket of soon-to-be-revealed stars, Lisa, Oliver, Abigail, and Ethan forged the first links in a chain of cherished routines—a testament to their collective resilience and the love that would carry them through whatever lay ahead.

Sunlight filtered through the kitchen window, casting a warm glow on the assortment of craft supplies spread across the dining table. With a contented smile, Lisa watched as Abigail and Ethan chose their favorites from the pile. She handed each of them a large piece of poster board, their blank canvases for the vision boards that would capture their dreams.

"Okay, guys," she began, her voice soft but filled with an undercurrent of excitement. "Think about what you love to do, the things that make you happy. We'll find activities here that let you explore those interests."

Abigail's fingers danced over the colored markers before selecting a bright purple one. "I wanna draw," she declared, her eyes shining with the thought of art classes where she could bring her imagination to life.

"Then we'll sign you up for the Saturday morning art workshop at the community center," Lisa said. She wrote "Art Workshop" on a sticky note and handed it to Abigail, who pressed it firmly onto her board.

Ethan peered over his glasses at Oliver, who stood ready with a stack of local brochures. "What about you, buddy?" Oliver asked, a hint of eagerness in his tone.

"Um... baseball?" Ethan's voice was tentative, but his eyes held a spark of genuine interest.

"Baseball it is," Oliver replied, his eyes reflecting pride. "There's a little league team that practices at the park. You'll hit home runs in no time." He scribbled "Little League" on another note and passed it to Ethan, who placed it next to a cut-out picture of a baseball mitt.

"What if I'm no good at it?"

Lisa glanced between them, her heart swelling with a cocktail of emotions—pride, hope, and a fierce determination to support their passions. She reached across the table, squeezing their hands gently. "You'll both be amazing," she assured them.

As the afternoon waned, they continued to work on their vision boards. Pictures of nature trails, fishing rods, and musical instruments joined the collage of aspirations. Laughter and chatter filled the room as they shared stories of past experiences and future hopes.

"Look at this," Ethan said, pointing to a photo of the northern lights he had found in a magazine. "Can we see these?"

"Absolutely," Lisa replied, remembering her sense of wonder the first time she saw the aurora borealis dance across the sky. "We'll plan a night to go out and watch them together."

"Can I put it on the board?" Abigail asked, her eyes gleaming with the promise of celestial wonders.

"Of course," Lisa said, helping her to place the image among the others carefully.

They stepped back to admire their collective handiwork, the vision board now a colorful mosaic of their unified dreams. Oliver wrapped his arms around Lisa from behind, resting his chin on her shoulder. Together, they looked at the hopeful faces of Abigail and Ethan, seeing not only the reflection of their newfound family but also the boundless potential of the days ahead.

"And what about you, Lisa?" Oliver suddenly asked.

"What about me?" she said, puzzled.

"What's on your vision board?" he asked.

"Ah, nonsense," she said. "I don't have one."

"Come on, Mom," Ethan said. "You must have something you dream of doing?"

"Yeah," Oliver chimed in. "What's your dream? I seem to remember you telling me of one when we were in the woods, remember?"

"What is it, Mommy?" Abigail said. "What is it?"

Lisa smiled secretively, then wrote *Café* on the board. "There, are you happy?"

Oliver kissed her forehead gently. "Yes, very happy."

They carefully mounted their creation on the wall, its presence a silent vow of the adventures and growth to come. In the cozy embrace of their Alaskan home, amidst the laughter and shared dreams, they were more than just a family—they were a team ready to face the future, whatever it might hold.

After dinner, as Oliver and Lisa walked side by side through a forest path dusted with early snow, Lisa brought up the board again. She hadn't been able to stop thinking about it. The air around them was crisp, carrying the scent of pine and the promise of new beginnings.

"You know it's true that I've always wanted my own café," Lisa confessed, watching her breath form clouds in the chilly air. "A place of tranquility where people could come and feel at home."

"Then you should," Oliver encouraged, his eyes reflecting conviction.

"And you," Lisa nudged him playfully with her elbow, "you've talked about refurbishing that old boat shed down by the pier. You have a gift with wood-work, Oliver. It's time to share it with the world."

He smiled, a look that warmed her more than any coat ever could. "I miss the satisfaction of creating something with my own two hands. Maybe it's time I picked up my tools again."

Their shared laughter echoed in the stillness, mingling with the rustling of leaves and the distant call of a raven. They were two souls, once battered by life's storms, now finding refuge in each other's dreams. As the sun dipped below the horizon, casting hues of purple and orange across the sky, Lisa and Oliver walked on, their steps light and hopeful.

"Whatever we decide," Oliver said, wrapping an arm around her shoulders, "we'll do it together. That's what matters."

Lisa leaned into his embrace, her heart swelling with the excitement of possibilities. Here, in this quiet town cradled by wilderness, they were not just surviving—they were thriving. Together, they would weave their aspirations into the fabric of their lives, creating a tapestry rich with love and the colors of a future painted by their own hands.

Lisa stood on the porch, shivering slightly as the brisk Alaskan air nipped at her cheeks. She watched Oliver wrestle with a stubborn pile of firewood that refused to stack neatly. His breath misted in the cold, his hands emerging red and chafed from his gloves, yet there was a steadfast determination in the set of his jaw.

"Maybe we should just buy our wood pre-chopped this winter," Lisa suggested gently, hugging herself for warmth.

Oliver straightened, shaking his head with a chuckle. "And miss out on all this fun? Not a chance."

"Fun" wasn't the word she would have chosen, but she admired his perseverance. However, the unease inside her grew; this was about more than firewood—it was about their ability to tackle obstacles together.

"Oliver, we need to be realistic. There's enough to do around here without you playing lumberjack," she said, a hint of concern threading through her voice. "We also need to think about what the future looks like... if you really want to be out at sea all the time, away from all of us. Especially now with more people to join our little family soon...," she said, gently caressing her bulging stomach.

He paused, leaning on the ax, and met her gaze. Then he laughed wholeheartedly and lifted her in his arms. She squealed, and he put her down.

"Sorry. I might have been a little too enthusiastic."

"Enthusiastic is good," Lisa replied, a smile tugging at her lips. "But let's channel it into something that won't break your back."

That evening, they sat by the fireplace, the flames casting a warm glow over their faces. The children were tucked into bed, stories of arctic foxes and northern lights lingering in their dreams. Lisa and Oliver huddled close on the worn sofa, a notebook open between them as they plotted their future.

"What do you think about a workshop?" Oliver mused, tracing a line on the paper with his finger. "A place where I can do my woodworking, maybe sell some pieces...."

"That could be wonderful." Lisa imagined the cozy space filled with laughter and sawdust, locals asking him to create keepsakes with his own hands. "And I could start a small café next door—fresh coffee and homemade pastries. A little nook for book lovers."

Their ideas flowed, weaving together like the threads of a net, strong and supportive. Challenges arose—budgets, permits, renovations—but with each obstacle, they found a solution, their discussions punctuated by shared glances and understanding nods.

"I've got some money coming from the sale of my house in Seattle, and you have some saved; with that, we could get pretty far. At least it's a start."

"It sure is," Oliver said.

"Look at us," Lisa marveled, her hand finding Oliver's. We're planning a business, building a life, creating a new life. It's exciting."

"It's us," Oliver agreed with palpable excitement. "Whatever comes, we'll face it together."

The night deepened outside, stars twinkling above the slumbering town as if winking at the couple's audacity to dream. Inside, the fire cracked and popped, its dance reflecting in their eyes—a testament to their resilience and passion.

"Tomorrow," Lisa whispered, her heart swelling, "we start making it happen."

"Tomorrow," Oliver echoed, sealing their pact with a kiss, the embers of their love and ambition glowing bright against the encroaching darkness.

The ribbon fluttered to the ground, soft blue against the crunch of fresh snow. Lisa's breath misted in front of her as she and Oliver stepped through the doorway of their new venture—a testament to dreams realized. The sign above, "The Seabreeze Café," glistened with the touch of morning frost, catching the first light of dawn in a hopeful glimmer.

"Can you believe it?" Lisa whispered, squeezing Oliver's hand. They stood together on the threshold, the warmth of the café spilling out onto the wooden porch. Her stomach was huge by now, and she knew it wouldn't be long before their little girl would join them.

"Believe it? I'm living it," Oliver replied, his eyes reflecting a pride that was as much for her achievements as his own. His arm found its way around her, drawing her close against him.

"Every nail, every cup of coffee it's all been worth it."

Inside, the café buzzed with the energy of their opening day. The scent of cinnamon and roasted coffee beans wrapped around them, a sensory embrace promising comfort and community. Scattered laughter from the early patrons filled the room, mixing with the chime of the door as others entered, curious and eager.

"Mom! Look!" Abigail's excited shout pulled Lisa's gaze to where her daughter stood by the display of homemade pastries, her face alight with wonder. Ethan was not far behind, his young hands carefully arranging the carved wooden figures Oliver had made —each a tiny milestone.

"Everything looks perfect, sweetheart." Lisa's voice carried the warmth of the oven-baked treats, her eyes shining with unshed tears. She watched her children take ownership of this new chapter in their lives, her heart swelling with maternal pride and boundless love.

"Let's take a picture!" Oliver suggested, retrieving his phone from behind the counter, his bearded face breaking into an easy grin. They huddled together among the rustic décor of their joint creation, the walls adorned with photographs of the coastline and shelves stocked with local crafts. The shutter's click captured the moment—a snapshot of triumph and shared joy.

As the day waned and the final customers filed out beneath the glow of the "Open" sign, Lisa and Oliver remained side by side, tidying up with contented sighs.

"Remember our first walk along the shore?" Lisa murmured, pausing to lean on the counter, holding her stomach, the flour residue from a successful bake still dusting her hands.

"Of course," Oliver chuckled, wiping down tables. "You were so guarded, yet so determined. Look how far we've come since then."

"Thanks to you," Lisa said, her voice a soft melody

of gratitude. "You gave me strength when I thought I had none left."

"Lisa, we gave each other strength," he corrected gently, coming to stand before her. He lifted her chin, encouraging her to meet his gaze. "We're a team—in business, in life, and in love."

"Here's to our next adventure," she toasted, raising an imaginary glass. Her smile was a light, guiding them toward a future of infinite possibilities.

"Whatever it may be, we'll embrace it together, forever and always," Oliver affirmed, leaning in to kiss her forehead—a seal over a silent vow they'd made long ago.

Their reflections danced in the windowpane, two silhouettes framed against the backdrop of an Alaskan twilight, the sky ablaze with ribbons of pink and orange. It was a scene etched in tranquility and expectation, an endearing pause before the rush of tomorrows yet to unfold.

And that's when Lisa felt it. The flush of wetness rushed from her body, leaving a pool of water below.

It was time for their next big adventure.

The End

Are you desperate to find out what happens to Lisa and Oliver next?

Get the second heart warming and captivating installment in the series, ***The One That Got Away*** on ***Amazon.com.***

"When a woman from Oliver's past shows up holding the hand of a young boy, Lisa and Oliver's love is once again tested... will they be able to overcome a storm threatening to tear them apart?
This book will have you turning the pages late into the night"